H. F Wallace

A Busy Life

A Tribute to the Memory of the Reverend David A. Wallace

H. F Wallace

A Busy Life
A Tribute to the Memory of the Reverend David A. Wallace

ISBN/EAN: 9783337402228

Printed in Europe, USA, Canada, Australia, Japan

Cover: Foto ©Raphael Reischuk / pixelio.de

More available books at **www.hansebooks.com**

A Busy Life:

A TRIBUTE TO THE MEMORY

OF THE

REV. DAVID A. WALLACE, D.D., LL. D.,

First President of Monmouth College.

BY THE

REV. H. F. WALLACE.

"I have fought a good fight, I have finished my course, I have kept the faith : henceforth there is laid up for me a crown of righteousness, which the Lord, the righteous judge, shall give me at that day ; and not to me only, but unto all them also that love His appearing."—II Tim. 4 : 7, 8.

GREELEY, COLORADO :
1885.

TO THE

ALUMNI OF MONMOUTH COLLEGE,

WHO REPRESENT

THE CAUSE OF CHRISTIAN EDUCATION,

FOR WHICH MONMOUTH COLLEGE WAS FOUNDED,

AND TO WHICH THE SUBJECT OF THESE

MEMOIRS HAD CONSECRATED HIS

LIFE, THIS VOLUME IS

DEDICATED.

CONTENTS.

PART I--IN MEMORIAM.

PART II—DEAD, YET SPEAKING.

(v)

Preface.

IT is with feelings of diffidence that I present this
volume to the public. Few will, perhaps, see
more defects than myself. Yet I feel that it is going
among friends—among those who knew Dr. Wallace,
and who desire some memorial of him. This, however, can be but a feeble one. His lasting memorial
is written upon the hearts of the sons and daughters
of Monmouth College. I therefore send this volume,
not into the cold, cynical world, to be judged by
merciless critics, but I send it especially to those
who knew him, and had learned to love him, and
who will refrain from passing a critical judgment.

The difficulty of gathering material for such a work
as this can only be known by those who have themselves undertaken a similar task. His busy life left
him no time for writing long letters, only short business ones, and very little in the form of a diary. In
1873 his residence was destroyed by fire, and most
of his manuscript sermons and lectures were burned.
Very few of his sermons, in later years, were written
in full. The matter from which choice was made for
Part II. was consequently limited.

To the many friends to whom I am indebted for

valuable materials, acknowledgment has been made in the course of the work where their communications have been used; but I would especially mention the names of Prof. J. C. Hutchison, Ph. D., a professor in Monmouth College almost from the beginning, who contributed the second chapter; the Rev. Marion Morrison, D. D. ,a classmate and life-long friend; the Rev. Alex. Young, D. D., LL. D., a colleague in two pastorates; the Rev. Hugh Forsythe, the Rev. J. T. Cooper, D. D., and the Rev. J. A., Grier. I would also acknowledge the many encouraging words that have come to me especially from the early alumni of Monmouth College.

My aim has been to present as truly as possible the inner life of the man; with the material at hand this could only be imperfectly done. There was much in the home life, and in the private communications with those with whom he had to deal, that can not be brought to the view of the public.

My prayer is that this little volume may be the means of magnifying the grace of God, that so cheered and sustained the heart of our departed brother, and of which he loved so much to speak to others.

GREELEY, COLO.,
  August 1, 1885.

PART FIRST.

IN MEMORIAM.

CHAPTER I.

David Alexander Wallace was born near Fairview, Guernsey County, Ohio, June 16, 1826. His ancestors belonged to that sturdy race—the Scotch-Irish —who left Scotland and settled in the district in Ireland called Ulster. They inherited largely the peculiar characteristics of the two countries. They carried with them wherever they went, a love of liberty—religious and secular; and were strong advocates of education. They figured largely in the American struggle for independence; and "the common schools of America, and the colleges were in a great measure inaugurated by them." The thought of separating religion from secular education never entered their minds. The Shorter Catechism, as well as the Bible, occupied a prominent place in their schools. They were educators in the highest sense of the word. They believed that secular education should be sanctified and directed by a knowledge of the things pertaining to the kingdom of God. They held that Christian statesmen were the safest and best to control the affairs of state, and

(3)

that men trained in the fear of the Lord made the best and most patriotic citizens.

David Wallace and John McClenahan were the grandfathers of David Alexander. It is not known when David Wallace came to this country; John McClenahan came in the year 1812, just before the declaration of war between the United States and England. The vessel in which he and his family came, was the last to enter an American port until after the cessation of hostilities. David Wallace is said to have been a man of sterling integrity, great equanimity of temper, and strong mental powers. He held the office of Justice of the Peace for about thirty years, or as long as he could be induced to accept it. He was a ruling elder in the Associate Reformed Church, first at St. Clairsville, Ohio, and afterwards at Fairview, Ohio.

John McClenahan was a ruling elder in the Fairview congregation for about thirty years. He possessed strong mental powers, a good memory and a great taste for reading, and thus secured a vast fund of information upon the history of the church. He wrote a number of articles for the press, some of which appeared in "The Preacher," now "The United Presbyterian."

John Wallace, the father of David Alexander, was born in Belmont county, Ohio. His mother, Jane McClenahan, was born in county Down, Ireland.

She was eight years of age when her parents came to America. They were married. June 14. 1825. when they settled on a farm near Fairview. John Wallace was a ruling elder in the Fairview congregation of the Associate Reformed Church for over twenty years: first under the pastoral care of the Rev. Samuel Findley. D. D.. afterward under that of the Rev. Hugh Forsythe. He died April 20. 1850. His pastor, the Rev. Hugh Forsythe, writes: " He was a man of good sense. sound judgment. very judicious and very prudent. He was kind hearted. In cases of discipline, if he erred at all. it was on the side of mercy. I suppose he had more influence over me than any other member of session. He had great influence in the congregation. Two things gave him influence in congregational meetings. good sense and a perfect willingness to do his part. He befriended a great many poor people. without respect to race or color. When he was buried, some colored people, whom he had befriended. were standing near the grave looking into it while tears were rolling down their cheeks. John Wallace was emphatically the poor man's friend."

His grandmother McClenahan. and mother. were women greatly beloved by all who knew them. They were respected and loved by their children and grandchildren. Their influence over their children was great. His mother, left a widow with a number of children, who were unable to do much for their own support, and with limited means, was compelled to plan and work for their support and education. But her cheerful spirit and energy carried her over all the difficulties in her way. The writer, though young during those trying years, can never forget the anxiety she manifested for the welfare of her children; and the thoughts that passed through his mind, when, morning and evening, we were gathered together, a chapter was read, and prayer was offered by her. This was in the days when women were unaccustomed to take any part in public religious exercises. She still lives, having attained her four-score years.

At an early age David Alexander manifested an aptness for learning, which led his parents to determine to give him an education. He started to school at the age of four years. It was in the winter of 1830. He spent that winter with his grandfather, Wallace. Although too young to walk to school through the snow, yet so desirous was he to attend that his uncles carried him there and back. At the age of twelve years he entered Madison College, located at Antrim, Ohio. He remained but a short time. His parents were unable to keep him at college continuously; hence he was under the necessity of teaching. He taught his first school at Green-wood, near his home, when he was about fifteen

years of age. A debating club was organized in
the neighborhood, which he attended, and in whose
exercises he took part. Here was manifested that
ability in debate which characterized him in after
years.

During 1842 1844 he was assistant in an academy
in West Virginia. His uncle, the Rev. William
Wallace, D. D., was nominally the principal, but
the work was mainly performed by his assistant. In
the autumn of 1844, he entered the junior class in
Miami University. The Rev. Marion Morrison,
D. D., who was a class-mate, and much of the time
room-mate, thus writes concerning his college days:
"He made many warm friends while in college.
He was the kind of student who will always command the respect of his professors. Very diligent
and intensely devoted to his studies, he never went
into the recitation room without having made
thorough preparation, unless something very unusual
occurred. Then he plainly told the professor he
was not prepared, and gave the reason. He was not
satisfied with a recitation unless he had thoroughly
mastered the subject. He was ambitious, but his
ambition was of that kind which led him to make
thorough work of whatever he undertook. His
temperament was such that sometimes he was the
most jubilant; then again he would be much cast
down, almost despondent. Yet when in his most

despondent mood he was able to work on with such
energy, that no one, not on intimate terms with him,
would ever suspect his discouragements. This
remained with him during life."

He graduated in August, 1846, at the age of
twenty, with the honors of his class. While in the
last session of the senior year, he was elected president of Muskingum College, at New Concord, Ohio.
This position he held until 1849, when he resigned
the presidency of the college, and accepted the position of principal of the North Ward Public School
of Wheeling, West Virginia, which position he held
about two years.

In these positions he was fitting himself for his
life work, that of an educator. But his desire was
to secure a theological education, and to this end
his heart was turned, and his energies were bent.
While at Wheeling, he pursued a course of private
study in theology, under the direction of his uncle,
Dr. William Wallace. He spent two sessions at the
Theological Seminary. The first at Oxford, Ohio,
then under the direction of the Rev. Joseph Claybaugh, D. D.; and the second at Allegheny, under
the direction of the Rev. John T. Pressly, D. D.
He was licensed by the Second Associate Reformed
presbytery of Ohio, April 10, 1849. He attended
the seminary at Allegheny after his licensure. About
this time he received a call from Canonsburg, Pa.;

also one from the congregation of Fall River, Mass.; but he felt it his duty to accept the latter, although the more needy and less inviting field. He was ordained by the Associate Reformed presbytery of New York, and installed pastor of the Fall River congregation, June 3, 1851.

He spent the summer previous to his ordination in this congregation. In a letter to his friend, Marion Morrison, he gives expression to his feelings in reference to the work in which he was engaged, in these words: "It has been my lot heretofore to be compelled to work. I have got into the way of it I can't keep from it—work I must. How do you find it? Is not preaching to souls a very serious business, far different than seminary preaching? Oh, how awful a business! What earnest minister would think of decking his sermons with garlands, made of the flowers of rhetoric? For my part, I feel that the work is too awful for any such trifling. I talk right on the plainest truths of the word-naked though they be. I would not polish a truth, gloss it up, until it slips down like an oyster or a sugar coated pill; the rough corners sometimes make the impression." In this connection we will insert an extract from an article of the Rev. James A. Grier, which shows that his early ideas of preaching clung to him through life. "His presentation of truth was so exceedingly clear and simple that often it did not look well in print. In the pulpit, from his lips, it was the great power of God. In all the branches of illustration, he was a master. Especially was he at home in analogies drawn from ordinary life, travel, business transactions and such like matter of fact affairs. What clear, pungent illustration of expiation and substitution and the duty of complete repentance he used to draw from the ordinary occurrences of human life, and all presented in the most idiomatic English. He never lacked a word or apt phrase, but it was always clean and chaste. He was deficient in the mental qualities which produce floridity in eloquence, and which takes delight in elaborate ornamentation. Yet he had a sublimity about him, which lifted him into lofty heights at times; and at such times the thought and speech of the man did not alone seem to rise but the man himself. Such occurrences were somewhat rare, and the flights short, but his strokes were those of the eagle. He had large power of pathos, although he rarely showed it. I remember a chapel sermon on ‘Looking to Jesus,’ when almost every face was wet with weeping, and another on the ‘Solace there is in Jesus at the time of death,’ when some of the audience broke out in sobs. At such times his soul seemed in flame with a divine fervor.”

In reference to his work in Fall River, previous to his installation, he said: ‘‘I have to work very hard here. I am as emphatically a missionary as though I were in Damascus. I go from house to house preaching; prayer meeting and lecture on Wednesday evening, two sermons on Sabbath, a lecture on the Shorter Catechism on Sabbath evening, complete the round of my parochial labors. It keeps me busy—busy, but that I like." Concerning his work in Fall River while pastor, we have been furnished the following: " In addition to his abundant services on the Sabbath, he conducted a Bible class on Tuesday evening, which was open to all who desired to attend. Thursday evening was devoted to the weekly prayer meeting. He always gave a lecture, taking as a basis one of the questions in the Shorter Catechism. When he came, he found a congregation discouraged and downcast, by means of disappointment and debt. The congregation was divided into districts. An elder was assigned to take charge of a district and be a leader in it. They met once a week to talk over the sermon of the previous Sabbath, and for prayer and praise. The pastor met with one of these divisions each week. There was also a plan for work among those who did not attend any church. Those who were at work under this plan reported once a month, at his study, their progress and any work of interest."

We here give an incident which illustrates his work and the character of his preaching. It is one of those experiences which the Master gives to his faithful servants to encourage them in their work. While he was living at Wooster, he received a letter from a man whom he had never seen, nor did he know anything concerning him. The writer stated that, years before, he had been in Fall River, had been living a very careless life. Being in the park, in the suburbs, one Sabbath evening, where a young man was preaching in the open air, he was attracted by the "handsome boyish face of the preacher." who was presenting the free offer of salvation. which he was enabled to accept. He ascertained the name of the young man. but lost sight of him, yet he never forgot that face. He had at that late date learned where he was. and had been constrained to write and tell him he had been instrumental in saving his soul. "In the morning sow thy seed, and in the evening withhold not thine hand: for thou knowest not whether shall prosper, either this or that, or whether they both shall be alike good."

In 1853 he was elected to succeed the Rev. Dr. Claybaugh, as Professor of Theology, in the Associate Reformed Theological Seminary at Oxford, Ohio; he had also been chosen to fill the chair of mathematics in the Miami University, located at the same place. Upon the advice of his presbytery. these offers were declined, as was also a call from one of the churches at Pittsburgh.

Previous to this time, August 21, 1851, he had been united in marriage to Miss Martha J. Findley, daughter of Mr. James Findley, of New Concord, Ohio, who proved a faithful companion and helper through all the trying scenes of his life.

A mission station had been started in East Boston, and at the request of his presbytery, he resigned his charge at Fall River, to engage in the work at that place. He commenced labor in this field on the last Sabbath of January, 1854. The congregation was regularly organized August 16, 1854, and he was installed pastor November 15th of the same year. The work at East Boston was much of the same character as that at Fall River. Many of the members were young men, who worked in the ship-yards. The work among these was much enjoyed. Nevertheless the work of building up a congregation was arduous and slow.

He enjoyed a great advantage in having access to the public libraries of Boston, and by hard and systematic study he was enabled to prepare himself for work in after years. In addition to his regular pastoral duties, he prepared and published a pamphlet, entitled "The Theology of New England; An attempt to exhibit the doctrine now prevalent in the Orthodox Church of New England." Dr. Daniel Dana, of Newburyport, Mass., in an introduction to this pamphlet, says: "The worthy and respected author of this pamphlet has executed a task of no common importance. He has presented to the churches a view of the theology of New England, as it now exists, together with the means and steps by which it has arrived at its present position. The whole work is marked with great care and accuracy of investigation, with great clearness of statement, and with a candor which is mingled with a decided and warm attachment to the pure principles of gospel truth. In a work involving such extensiveness of general survey, and such minute statement of particulars, it would be strange indeed, were there to be found no mistakes. In the present case, it is believed, there are few, and these of small importance."

This pamphlet shows the influence which surrounded orthodox ministers of the Calvinistic school, and exhibits the difficulties they had to encounter in building up a congregation of the Calvinistic faith. These doctrines he firmly believed. He believed them, not because they were the doctrines of his church, or of his fathers, but believed them because, upon thorough investigation, he found them to be in harmony with the Word of God. Before this, while a student, he went over this system in comparison with Arminianism. He had found himself inclined to Arminianism and wrote to his uncle, the Rev. James M. Henderson, pastor of an Asso-

ciate congregation in Indiana, stating his difficulties.
Perhaps he had known that his uncle had, when a
young man, stumbled for years on the same ground,
and could therefore help him in his difficulty. He
replied in a series of twelve letters, which led him
to embrace the Calvinistic system of doctrine. It
was his design to have these letters published, but
before it was accomplished, these with other valuable papers, were destroyed by fire. He did not
want to believe and profess simply what his parents
professed, without examining for himself and knowing why he thus believed. He, however, did not
lightly esteem the opinions of his fathers. In later
years he endeavored to impress upon the minds of
his students the importance of adhering to the faith
of their fathers until, after a thorough personal
examination, they were satisfied they were mistaken.
It was well that he had the opportunity to go over
and settle thoroughly in his own mind these important fundamental truths; for afterwards his time was
so much occupied with pressing college duties that he
would scarcely have had the opportunity. He afterwards frequently remarked, that he could not have
sustained himself in Monmouth during these active,
busy years, if it had not been for what he had garn-
ered in Boston.

He had been laboring in East Boston nearly two
years, when he received an invitation from the Board

of Trustees of Monmouth College, Monmouth, Illinois, to become the president of that newly founded institution. So reluctant was he to leave his present field, that he at first declined the invitation. However, the health of Mrs. Wallace had been failing; the climate of New England was too severe for her. In the winter and spring of 1856, her lungs gave her much trouble. Under these circumstances an invitation came the second time to become president of Monmouth College. He consulted with a noted physician, a specialist in lung disease, who was very emphatic in his opinion that she could not live in that climate. This decided him to accept the position tendered him in Monmouth College. His resignation of the pastoral charge of the East Boston congregation was accepted by the presbytery, September 10, 1856, and soon after he went to Monmouth to commence what proved to be the great work of his life.

CHAPTER II.

The history of David Alexander Wallace would be but half told if it did not include in its telling his relations with Monmouth College. Indeed, we, who were the most intimately acquainted with the college and her president, had begun to think that they were inseparable—the one could not exist without the other—and, when compelled to consent to a separation, we yielded to the will of a Divine Power that knew best. · And this relation was formed at such an early day in the history of the college, that a brief account of its origin will be necessary to complete the story.

The thought of establishing Monmouth College originated in the minds of men who felt the need of a Christian school of learning. The first public step taken for the establishment of such a school was in the action of the Second Associate Reformed presbytery of Illinois, in 1853, by which the following persons were appointed trustees of the "Academy," or High School, to be established at Monmouth under the direction of said presbytery, viz: Revs. J. C. Porter, W. R. Erskine and R. Ross.

2   (17)

Messrs. J. C. McCreary. W. R. Jamison, N. A. Rankin, E. C. Babcock, J. G. Madden. Dr. J. A. Young. Hon. A. C. Harding and Judge James Thompson.

The Board of Trustees of Monmouth Academy was organized May 9, 1853, by electing Rev. J. C. Porter president and Hon. James Thompson secretary and treasurer. A building committee was appointed and immediate steps taken to procure a suitable building; but no permanent one was secured until 1856, until which time the academy was conducted, first in the Christian church, then in the basement of the Presbyterian church, and afterwards in a district school-house.

Monmouth Academy was opened on the first Monday in November, A. D. 1853, with the reading of the Scriptures and prayer, with Rev. James R. Brown as principal, and Miss M. S. Madden, first assistant teacher. Rev. Brown continued in charge of the school as its efficient principal until January 1, 1856, at which time a full faculty was elected, and Monmouth College inaugurated.

The organization of a complete college faculty was effected by the election of Rev. D. A. Wallace, President; Rev. J. R. Brown, Professor of Languages, and Rev. Marion Morrison, Professor of Mathematics. The school as an academy and college was under the care of the Second Associate Reformed presbytery of Illinois. until October. 1856, when, at the meeting of the Associate Reformed Synod of Illinois, it was, at the request of the presbytery, taken under the care of the synod and entrusted, in its government, to a Board of Trustees, consisting of twenty-four members, eighteen to be elected by the synod—including those already in office elected by the Second Associate Reformed presbytery—and six to be elected by the Board of Trustees itself. Thus Monmouth College organized first as an academy, then changed into a college, was ready for faculty and students.

The Rev. David A. Wallace, at this time pastor of the East Boston Associate Reformed Mission Church, having been chosen President, with Rev. Marion Morrison, an esteemed classmate at Miami University, Professor of Mathematics, and Rev. J. R. Brown, the former principal, Professor of Latin, came to Monmouth in February, 1856, to visit the field with a view of considering the question of accepting or declining the offer of president of the incipient college.

He returned to his home in East Boston, and, after consulting his wife—a thing he always did before deciding an important question of life—he decided to accept. He was led to this conclusion largely by the health of his wife, who could not stand the stormy sea-breezes, and her physician advised a change of climate. Demitting his charge in East Boston, he left for the West in September, and reached Monmouth in October, 1856.

The college opened in September, as announced, with Professor Morrison acting president until the arrival of Dr. Wallace. He came in October, as we have said, and at once entered upon the work of his life—the establishment of a Christian college in the West. Filled with this purpose, he left his home in in the East and came West, and entered on the work with an energy and zeal that knew no abatement until compelled to seek a rest from his labors, first, in a short vacation granted him in 1868, which he spent in Europe; then in a brief visit to the seashore in 1876, and finally in an entire separation from the child of his heart—Monmouth College. The faculty carried on their work with Dr. Wallace added to their number; and though the students were not up to the standard of advancement for college classes, with God's blessing on their efforts, they hoped soon to rise to the stature of a full-grown college.

The first year closed and the first annual catalogue was issued. It contained the names of ninety-nine students as having been in attendance, four of whom were ready for the junior class, four for the sophomore, and seven for the freshman. To give some conception of the thought that was in the mind and heart of this good man and his fellow laborers, concerning their work, we quote from the pages of this catalogue the article on the "Religious Instruction" of the students:—

All the students are required to attend the worship of God daily in the College chapel, and to recite a Bible lesson once a week. All are likewise required to attend public worship and Bible class in some church on the Sabbath. Those who take a full course will read, exegetically, the greater part of the New Testament in Greek, and select portions of the Old Testament in Hebrew. In addition to studying the usual text-books on Natural Theology, Evidences of Christianity, and Moral Philosophy, they will take a brief course in the principles of the Gospel, as set forth in Hodge's "Way of Life." This course of religious instruction will be especially valuable to those whose professional studies will not lead them to a careful examination of the facts and principles of the Word of God. A students' prayer-meeting has been organized. It is well attended. The Faculty regard it as an important part of their work to labor for the moral and spiritual welfare of the students.

A charter was obtained in February, 1857, and Dr. Wallace was inaugurated president September 1, 1857. President Jonathan Blanchard, of Knox College, gave an introductory address on "The Course of Study in American Colleges;" Rev. J. C. Porter, president of the Board of Trustees, gave a brief history of the rise and progress of the college; Rev. A. Nesbit gave the charge to the new president, and Dr.

Wallace delivered an inaugural address on "The Claims of the Bible as a Text-Book in the College Curriculum."

We have thus seen Monmouth College organized, the first year of its existence as a college finished, its first president inaugurated, and the subject of our memoir engaged in his chosen field of labor. His thoughts were first immediately directed to the welfare of the student. His moral interests were considered in the religious instruction provided in the curriculum of the college, as quoted above; in a weekly Bible lesson, and prayer-meeting, and preaching in the college chapel on the Sabbath; and in personal attention given the religious training of every student. Next, he applied himself to the course of instruction, which he aimed to make as complete as the standard of scholarship attainable by the students of that day would admit, and by advancing, year by year, to a still higher standard, finally to gain the excellence of scholarship given in the best colleges of the land.

Equally important with the work of instruction were the financial interests of the college, and to these he early and diligently applied himself, that they might be improved and enlarged. Feeling the necessity of changing the basis of scholarships, Professor Morrison was sent into the field, and accomplished, after faithful labors, a change of "Perpet-

ual Six-per-cent Scholarships" to "Twenty-five-year
Ten-per-cent Scholarships." And, again, to the
same end, Professor Ross was sent out, and succeeded
in increasing the college endowment fund ten thousand dollars by issuing college "script" for interest
on capital given.

Through the early days of his college life, the
subject of this memoir was father, instructor, pastor,
and friend of every student; and while he arranged
for the general charge of the literary work of the
college and its students, and controlled the financial
department of the institution, he neglected not the
personal welfare of every student. Each and all of
these felt that the president was his personal friend.
In the chapel on the Sabbath, he unfolded in plain,
practical sermons, the great principles of the Gospel
for the encouragement and building up in knowledge,
faith and righteousness the characters of the Christian students; while by the same means and by earnest personal appeal, he sought to lead the unwary
to Christ.

Again, we early find him mastering the details of
his college work in the "Class-books," "Monthly
Reports," and "Annual Record." When the writer
of this came into his connection with the college in
1858, he found the president himself keeping all the
records; and it required a year's apprenticeship of
good behavior to persuade to the transfer of the bur-

dens of this clerical work, so jealous was Dr. Wallace of all the interests of the college, and so thoughtful of the minutest details of its management. Thus,
in the earlier years of the college, our friend was
president, professor, financial agent, pastor, preacher,
tutor, and registrar.

While giving himself to the work in this whole-
hearted manner, the war came upon us, and, while
yielding to the inevitable, he carried out his oft-enun-
ciated motto: "We must educate in war as well as
in peace." He was ready for war or for peace. To
those who were prepared and willing to go to battle,
he said, "Go, and God bless you and keep you;" to
those whose plain duty it was to remain at home, he
said, "Stay and work, and gain higher planes of
knowledge, and enter upon that conflict whose wea-
pons are not carnal, but spiritual." During the dark
days of the war he was truly the soldier's friend,
encouraging him in preparations for the battle-field,
bidding him good-bye, and visiting him in camp.
Many of our students, having gone to Fort Donelson,
he went there to see them, taking with him many a
father's and mother's blessing for their boys. Well
do we remember the hearty applause given in the
college chapel, when, on his return, he related how
he was received by the boys in blue and by the commander at Fort Henry, to whom he went, on his way
South, and told him he was Dr. Wallace, on his way

to Fort Donelson to "see his boys." This commander ordered out a four-horse team and guard of cavalry to escort the Doctor across the country to Donelson.

With all this work resting upon him, he enters a new enterprise. The college was increasing in the number of students and in means to carry on its work of instruction to such an extent that the college building was not large enough, and so it was determined to erect a new one. The liberality of two of his firmest friends greatly encouraged them at the beginning of this work: A. Y. and David Graham purchased a quarter-section of land immediately east of the old town plot. This they laid out in lots, and offered as a donation to the college fund one-sixth of these lots. This liberal gift was accepted, and the lots were afterwards, by agreement with the donors, sold, and the proceeds transferred to the building fund. In this work Dr. Wallace was chairman of the building committee, collector and treasurer of the fund, and superintendent of the work of building. To complex and further increase his individual labors, the first contractors gave up their contract; the building committee then undertook to complete the work themselves, and did so at a saving of one thousand dollars on the original contract.

Dr. Wallace had the great burden of the oversight

of this building work. He solicited the subscriptions, collected the funds, kept the accounts, superintended the work, and even attended to the payment of the workmen. Humanly speaking, he could never have succeeded in this enterprise, had not God in His providence given him such men as Judge Quinby, C. Hardin, A. Y. Graham, J. G. Madden, and Judge Thompson, to counsel. encourage, and fill his coffers, so that every Saturday night he was able to pay his workmen for the week's labor. And thus we entered our new building May 3, 1863.

The building committee gave the president. for his valuable services in superintending the erection of the building. a lot on East Broadway street, which was exchanged for one donated to the college by A. Y. Graham, northeast of the college. On this lot Dr. Wallace built a dwelling. and occupied it until it was destroyed. accidentally, by fire in 1875.

Having finished the work of the college building, Dr. Wallace gave himself to the work of the college instruction and improving the college finances. In 1865 he undertook the task of raising $45,000. in order to secure an offered donation of $5,000 by Judge Quinby. This work was entered into with the determination of success, and success crowned his efforts. He traveled through Illinois, and eastward to and through New York, visiting congregations, individuals. preaching the Gospel, and pleading for the Lord's money to carry on the Lord's work, and, with happy heart, though wearied body, he rested from his labors, and reported $50,000 increase to the College Endowment Fund.

With his manifold labors in class-room and chapel, pulpit and field, country house and farm and treasurer's office and students' study, he gave way under the pressure and broke down in health. A vacation was granted him. The faculty provided for his classes, and in 1868 he sailed for the old country, where amid new scenes he rested a while from his college work and regained some of his wonted fire and vigor. He came back to us renewed in health and spirits, and entered with new hopes on his life-work. He had gone to rest from his labors in that land of history and song and college culture, and yet, as ever, his vacation was a season of study and investigation. For he returned with new ideas of college life which he incorporated into the curriculum and general management of the institution. Among these, were the "Honor Course," and change of the Board of Trustees and Executive Committee into the "College Senate," composed of Directors and Trustees, with the president of the college ex-officio president of the Senate.

Thus entering anew on the work, he continued it with unabated zeal for eight years more, until in 1876 his powers of endurance gave way under the stress of the burdens which his broad and willing shoulders carried. He sought to be relieved entirely from his work, and offered his resignation of college president to the Board; but it heeded not his cry of an over-taxed life, and granted him another rest. He went to Fall River, Massachusetts, where in the old field of his early ministerial labors, and contiguous to the soothing air of the sea, he sought relief, and gained health and strength.

Again he returned to the college and took up the burdens he had laid aside for a time. These he bore for one year, and had entered upon a second, which he was not able to complete. He offered his resignation a second time in December, 1877; and though we plead with him to withdraw it, offering to lighten his labors and increase his remuneration, we were compelled by him to accept it. And, thus, a wise president, a faithful preceptor, a kind father, a loving brother and a devoted friend, severed his connection with us. Still, though gone from us in the body, we ever felt that he was with us in spirit on the college rostrum, in the Monday evening prayer-meeting, in the chapel services and in the studies of professors and students. How many a white-winged messenger of love and friendship found its way to his home in Wooster, Ohio, whither he had removed, and many a heart-felt "God bless you," and wise counsel, when sought, came back on swift wings to gladden and rejoice the heart!

We ever felt that we had in our former president and co-laborer while he was alive, though absent from the council room and social circle, a faithful and loving friend. But, alas! His life-work was done. His Master claimed him and he left us sorrowing and sad for his untimely death, for the resignation of his stewardship on earth speedily followed his demission of the stewardship of Monmouth College.

As a college president, we regard Dr. Wallace as having few equals or superiors. This proposition leads to a consideration of what constitutes a college president, especially of a college constituted as is Monmouth, an institution consecrated to Christian education. For such a school, there is needed the faithful gospel preacher, the earnest Christian worker, the zealous pastor, the wise disciplinarian, the successful teacher, the skillful manager of affairs, the safe financier, the accurate scholar, the students' friend, the godly man. All these excellencies Dr. Wallace combined in his personal character in an eminent degree. That he was a faithful preacher, pastor and earnest Christian worker in the class-room and pulpit, Dr. Alexander Young thus testifies:

But the college and its means of training young men and women were dear to him only as the students were brought under influences which should make them Christian men and women, and formers of the characters and lives of others. His preaching and his teaching were always directed to that end. He never sought the reputation of a great theologian or a great orator. His pulpit teaching was singularly free from metaphysical and theological subtleties. The conversion, the instruction and the encouragement and strengthening of the faith and the increasing of the joy of the believer, were the great objects which he kept in view. Christ in his power and willingness to save, were the great themes in the pulpit, in the prayer-meetings, in the class-room and in dealing personally with students and inquirers.

In an article published in the *Evangelical Repository* for December, 1883, the Rev. James A. Grier, a pupil of Dr. Wallace. speaks with admiral clearness and force of the "Man and His Work." We make a brief extract from the portion bearing on the point in hand:

Rarely a Sabbath passed in which he did not address his classes upon some pertinent scriptural theme, and it was very likely to be some phase of repentance, faith, holiness, union with Christ, or some kindred topic. The sermons were not carefully prepared, but they were often exhaustive of the topic, and were delivered with great unction and power. It was partly in order to have an opportunity of preaching to the assembled college that he so long held the co-pastorate of the Second (United Presbyterian) Church. His preaching was the

channel of his greatest spiritual power over the
college. It dealt in the saving fundamentals of the
gospel of free grace. It had no discussion of
science or other problems, and was adapted to all
hearts. * * * * His endeavor was to
bring every student into the enjoyment of personal
salvation. Who of us does not remember his
appeals to hearts to yield themselves to the Saviour?
Who does not call to mind the Sabbath evening
appointments in some recitation room to meet with
any who had the slightest concern respecting their
own personal safety. and his plain unfolding, upon
such occasions, of the doctrine of trust in the Lord
Jesus? How many of us can recall appointments
with Christian students to meet for a quarter or a
half-hour before the Monday evening prayer-meeting. to beseech the throne of grace for the outpour-
ing of the Spirit upon the college? How often he
directed the attention of some one who professed
Christ to a fellow-student whom he wished to bring
into the family of God? As one thinks these old times
over, the memories of his concern for the salvation
of souls and his honest and wise endeavors therefor.
sweep him on the most profound conviction that here
was a man who loved the souls of his fellow-men as
made in the image of the Creator. and who loved
the kingdom of his Lord as it is established in
human spirits.

Few men in the United Presbyterian Church are
better qualified for speaking with authority regarding the fitness of other men for teachers and educators than Dr. J. R. Johnson. Long and famil-

iarly acquainted with Dr. Wallace, Dr. Johnson thus speaks of him in these regards:

In the death of Dr. Wallace, the cause of education has lost one of its best friends. There are men as deeply interested in the work as he. but only a few combine so great practical efficiency and enthusiasm with the power of passionately showing it forth. Some of his best years were given to college work. They were given, too, as not many knew how to give them. He was not only interested in his pupils, but he loved them. They were on his heart day and night. What he felt, he was able to impart and thus make others feel. No student went from him without carrying away more or less of his personality, and even the least credulous of them all could speak only of his goodness and power, in affectionate forgetfulness of anything like faults, and in generous praise of his virtues. The sorrow they feel and express, now that he is gone, is a tribute that death only now and then calls forth. In this way. so in many others. "he. being dead, yet speaketh."

Not the least among the many faculties possessed by Dr. Wallace in an eminent degree, and one which contributed no little to his remarkable success in college work. was his administrative abilities so far as the exercise of necessary discipline in college work is concerned. He held the secret of successful disciplinary regulation known to so few. On this matter. we can do no better than to allow Professor J. H. Wilson, the life-long friend and long co-laborer of Dr. Wallace, speak:

One striking characteristic of Dr. Wallace as a disciplinarian was in the large proportion of disciplinary work done outside and indirectly. For the maintenance of good conduct, the prevention of disorder, he depended largely upon the power of religious principle and the force of public example. Hence, in his class-room lectures, his chapel talks, in Christian Union, in Monday evening prayer-meeting, in Sabbath services—everywhere, he strove to enlighten the judgment and quicken the conscience of the pupil. And his knowledge of the human heart was so complete, his delineation so accurate, and his presentation so vivid, that the student would often feel as if his own individual case was under discussion. The earnest piety and sound public sentiment thus developed and cherished was a grand power in the work of government, checking many an outbreak and bringing back to honor and duty many a student inclined to break away from wholesome restraint. Another characteristic was the amount of private and individual work done. With the great mass of the students, the public and general work secured the desired end. But, as was to be expected, among so many young men and women there were always a few, sometimes a greater number, sometimes a less, who could not be reached and controlled by this general work. Indolence or perversity or vice had too strong a hold to yield readily to good influences. With wonderful quickness the characters of these were read and their propensities understood, and before they had time to form cliques and companies, they were made the objects of special care. In private

3

they were reasoned with, stimulated, encouraged, warned, admonished, as each special case seemed to need. Many an invitation was given to come to office or home where his influence was exerted.

These witnesses all testify to the exalted 'character of the man about whom we write, as a moral teacher. In the class-room, we regarded him as especially felicitous; his explanations were so plain and simple that the student readily and easily grasped the truth, and his analyses of the whole subject were so clear and accurate that only the most obdurate failed to learn. In the pulpit his method of instruction was the same; his propositions were clearly stated and the argument plain and pointed.

That he was a skillful financier of the college funds, the present sound financial system of the college plainly testifies. He inaugurated this system. The monthly statement of the treasurer to the Board of Trustees with the monthly supervision of his accounts and no bank system, is better adapted to protect the funds, and in all Dr. Wallace's personal care of any public funds in his hands an accurate account was always rendered.

The great power of President Wallace lay in his personal magnetism. Full of his work, he possessed the power of imparting the same enthusiasm in others; full of Christ, he was able by God's grace to bestow in a large degree, the same fullness to his co-laborers and pupils. It was this spirit which inclined the student to look on the president as his personal friend, and to see in that friend, the godly man, the Christian gentleman.

But his work in Monmouth College as its honored president, needs no eulogy from us to impress upon the church its influence and importance, and rank him who did it among the first college presidents of the land. It speaks for itself in its grand results. It is seen in the character of the school he founded, its liberal curriculum, in the thorough training it furnished the intellectual powers, in the minute details arranged by his acute mind for the conduct of its affairs in all its departments—instruction, execution, finance, from the care of the building to the supervision of the Senate—but above all, in the moral character of the instruction given, the training furnished for the development of the moral qualities of its students—in short, for the thorough training of every pupil of the college in the precepts of the Bible. He instituted a system in his Bible classes that if carried out by the students in after life, would give them a knowledge of the Bible scarcely less than that gained in a theological seminary. At the same time, he trained them to work for others as he worked for them. Instilling into them the spirit of enthusiasm which possessed his own soul, he cheered them on in their life-work.

The college founded in prayer as a Christian college for imparting Christian education and culture, was carried out by Dr. Wallace to the fullest extent of his abilities, consecrating his heart, mind and body to the great work of his life. The theme of his inaugural address in his induction to the office of president, was the "Claims of the Bible as a Text Book in the College Curriculum," and the noble utterances in that address but foreshadowed the work of his life. He defined education to be to fit man for accomplishing to some degree the end of his being, which end was to "glorify God and enjoy Him forever." Said he, "Shall the professor spend six days in the week in drilling the student in the principles of general literature and science and never once open the Bible to teach therefrom an infinitely higher knowledge than that to be found in any book of science and literature, a knowledge necessary to develop that moral excellence we have seen to be of such pre-eminent worth? No, no; a thousand times, NO! If they cannot do this without becoming sectarian, what then? Unhesitatingly and emphatically I answer, Let them be sectarian; sectarian a thousand times over rather than unchristian." He concluded this address in these words: "From out of one thousand of earnest hearts let daily petitions rise to our Father in Heaven that we all, Board of Trustees, faculty, students, may be blessed and made a blessing. That those who go forth from among us may be richly furnished with the most important wisdom and knowledge; that their powers may be developed by the highest culture; that above all they may be adorned with the beauty of holiness, eminently good and mighty to do good; that Monmouth College, be its students few or many, may be truly a Christian college." And to the close of his work in Monmouth College he labored faithfully and earnestly for that great end.

The fruits of his labors are to be seen in the character of the men and women who occupy important stations in life to-day and who owe much of their power to the wise, careful and patient training of the prime spirit of their alma mater.

One of these sons, Major R. W. McClaughry, at the memorial service in Monmouth, said, " Not only in our own land but in Egypt, India, Syria and the islands of the sea, are more than a hundred of these sons of Monmouth College making proof of their ministry, and of his faithfulness in their Christian education, besides the hundreds of men and women in other relations of life who by labors abundant and wide-reaching influence for good, are showing forth his teaching in their lives."

In concluding this memoir as it relates to Monmouth College, we would only add that this devotion was so absorbing that under it he consecrated

body, mind and heart to the work of his life. He
had but one object in accepting the place of president and that was to glorify God in establishing a
Christian college. To the accomplishment of this
end, he put forth every exertion, laboring day and
night with little or no cessation by way of vacation,
till nature gave way under the protracted strain, and
he was compelled to give the work to other hands.
He was unselfish to a marked degree, as the writer
saw him through twenty years of associated work.
He possessed a strong mind and a large heart, a
mind that looked after every detail and could reach
forward and grasp results, and a heart that was
generous, sympathetic, kind, tender and loving. It
was a heart that sought to embrace in its strong
affections every student of the college. And thus
all were bound to him by the cords of an abiding
love whose silken ties were never severed. And so
it was that, when over the wires was flashed the
intelligence that he was dead, the hearts of more
than five hundred sons and daughters of Monmouth
College mourned as for the loss of a beloved father.

CHAPTER III.

Monmouth College did not start with a full endowment bringing an income sufficient to pay a full corps of professors. The most rigid economy must be practiced, both in the number of professors employed and in the salaries paid. They must do extra work, and supplement their salaries from work outside. But such was their self-denying spirit, that this extra labor was cheerfully performed. The sons and daughters of to-day, as they are enjoying the comforts of their homes, do not, nor can they, value the self-denying toil of those who provided these homes for them. Neither can the sons and daughters of Monmouth College fully value the self-denying toil of those who labored to establish this institution. The question with them was not how large a salary they could obtain, but upon how little they could support their families in order that the college might live.

The Associate Reformed Church of Monmouth— now the First United Presbyterian—was organized May 9, 1853, and as yet they had not secured the services of a pastor. This position was offered to

David A. Wallace, when he signified his intention of accepting the presidency of the college, and was by him accepted. The work in this congregation comprised the usual work of a pastor. Indeed, the work of Dr. Wallace in Monmouth as a pastor may be briefly told. Concerning the work of an eminent minister of Scotland it was said, " When there are no battles the history of a country is brief and dull; but great is the happiness of the people. It is the same with the work and sphere of a Christian minister where he is faithful and the flock affectionate. The minister, loving and beloved, is felt everywhere as a rallying point and center of attraction. The beneficent machinery goes smoothly around, Christian charity lubricating every wheel; and, precisely, because everything is going on well, there is not much for the historian to tell." This was true in the pastorates of Dr. Wallace in Monmouth. The work of the college was the principal work. To this he bent all his energies; yet the work of the pastorate was conscientiously performed.

When the Theological Seminary at Oxford, Ohio, was removed to Monmouth, in 1858, Prof. Alexander Young, D. D., became associate pastor in the congregation. This arrangement continued until August, 23, 1860, when the Board of Trustees of the college desired the whole time of the president to be given to the college, both in teaching and in the interest of

the finances; consequently he was released. Concerning this period Dr. Young testifies thus: "Although he was released from all responsibility in the
congregation, yet he continued to exercise a constant
interest in its welfare, occasionally supplying its pulpit, and regularly attending its prayer-meetings and
the meetings of session, and in every practicable
way helping to promote its welfare: and as a member of the congregation his advice in business meetings and in other connections, was greatly to its advantage."

In December, 1863, the presbytery of Monmouth
granted the organization of the Second United Presbyterian Congregation of Monmouth. Services were
commenced in July, 1863, with Drs. Young and
Wallace as co-pastors. Arrangements were made to
combine the college service with the second service
of the congregation, which, in some measure light-
ened the labors of Dr. Wallace. "However, as responsibilities increased with the growth of the college, he felt that his sphere of labor needed concen-
tration. Monmouth College was founded with the
design of being, in an eminent degree, a Christian
college. The agencies for securing this end were
wisely arranged, president, professors and students
having definite and well-understood lines of effort
and influence. All had opportunities of influence on
all the students, and as officially their spiritual, as

well as their mental and moral instructor, his sphere was more extended and more comprehensive than that of any professor. Clearly seeing and valuing his work in this line, in order that all interested might receive the attention they required, and which he felt was his duty to give, shortly after his return from Europe, he requested to be released from all pastoral care in the affairs of the Second Church. The congregation consented to this request, and he was formally released by the presbytery December 29, 1868. However, the relations between the pastors, respecting their work and the college services in the afternoons of the Sabbaths, were continued as before. This co-pastorate, as co-equals in labor, duties and responsibilities, continued throughout six years, and in the modified form for two years longer; the pastor, the session and the people enjoying the co-operation and advice of Dr. Wallace in all ways which he could devise for their interest."

An impression being abroad in the church, that, on account of failing health. Dr. Wallace would be compelled to retire altogether from college work, efforts were made by different congregations to secure his services as pastor. In September, 1872, a unanimous call came to him from the Second United Presbyterian Congregation of Allegheny. Pa. There was also a movement started to elect him Professor of Pastoral Theology in the Theological Seminary at Allegheny. In reference to this call he says: "I have been weighing the question of acceptance. This morning I have set apart for the more careful consideration of it, and prayer for God's guidance. I have no desire but to know the mind of Christ. I am ready to submit to His will, and do His bidding, let it be what it may." After careful consideration, the call was declined. There were reasons which inclined him to accept. The call was made without any encouragement from him. He had absolutely declined to permit his name to be used. The movement to give him a position in the seminary was spontaneous, the money for the salary pledged, all without his knowledge. The work at Allegheny would have been all spiritual, a kind the most agreeable to him; while at Monmouth much would be mere secular work, a kind that was becoming more and more distasteful. In Allegheny there would be opened a very wide field of usefulness, the pastorate of a large congregation, and a professorship in the seminary. But, in addition to this, he would have a much larger income, which, in his peculiar circumstances, was of no little weight. But, over against all these was the conviction that the work to which he had been called in Monmouth, and to which he had consecrated himself, was not completed, and he must therefore remain.

Another call came to him in November, 1874, from

the United Presbyterian Congregation of St. Louis,
Mo. Concerning this call we give an extract from a
Monmouth paper, which shows the estimation from
a secular stand-point of his work in Monmouth:

It will be startling news to many of our citizens
that President Wallace contemplates leaving our city,
of which he has been an honored resident for so
many years. It seems almost incredible, since the
President has grown to be considered a permanent
and essential feature of the city, and whose departure has been an undreamed-of bereavement. It is
impossible, however, to conceal from our senses the
present *probabilities* that he will be induced to leave
us. He has received from the United Presbyterian
Congregation of St. Louis a call to become their
pastor, with an offer of a salary of $3,000 and a
parsonage. The congregation have just built a new
church and parsonage, and paid for them, and have
$20,000 in the treasury. So the call may be consid-
ered an inducement pecuniarily.

President Wallace will doubtless be inclined to
accept the call on several considerations. The labors,
cares, and responsibilities of his present position
are too onerous, and are weighing him down. The
worry and mental strain are becoming too much, even
for him. Under the change he would be relieved of
the great burden of this, and it is not strange that
he regards the proposition favorably. For eighteen
years he has been laboring ceaselessly and successfully in our midst, enduring much that was unpleas-
ant, vexatious, and trying, and receiving for his un-
tiring efforts a paltry consideration. He owes a duty

to himself and family as well as to others, and as he
is becoming advanced in years, the necessity of pro-
viding for the future forces itself upon him. His
present salary is $1,800 and a residence, barely suffi-
cient for economical support. When we reflect that
he has been struggling here for a score of years,
and has not even secured a home, we may reasonably
be surprised that he has not accepted a position from
among the frequent and generous offers that he has
hitherto received. He has too often, unselfishly,
drowned his own good in a regard for that of others.
When an Allegheny pastorate was tendered him some
time ago, the college Board offered to raise his salary
$700, but he refused it, not. however, because he did
not need it. but because the Board blindly offered
that which they did not have. Still he remained,
although a regard for his own comfort and welfare
would have prompted him to go to Allegheny.

This call was declined; the main reason which influenced him in his decision was the same that induced him to decline the call from Allegheny two
years before. He always loved the pastorate. It
was a great source of trial that he was compelled to
do so much secular work—work not intimately connected with the spiritual interests of Christ's kingdom. For this reason he was always ready to preach
wherever desired, and the vacant neighboring congregations frequently called upon him to supply their
pulpits. In 1872 the congregation of Henderson,
six miles from Monmouth, became vacant. After a

year of supplies they became discouraged, and fears of disorganization were felt. They desired Dr. Wallace to preach for them for a few months. This he consented to do, hoping that the salary he would thus receive would be a benefit to him, and he would thereby be enabled to release the college from paying the full amount promised him as president. He also entertained the hope that a change of labor, and the exercise it would require of him in the open air would be of advantage. From this arrangement the college was benefited financially, but whether he himself derived any personal benefit is doubtful. The extra expense that this arrangement required about consumed the additional income, and the exposure in inclement weather perhaps counteracted the benefits derived. Nevertheless, he willingly undertook the work and uncomplainingly did what he could for the people who called him to service, and rejoiced with them in their returning prosperity. After laboring with them for about a year, a call was presented to him, asking him to become their regular pastor, which was accepted December 22, 1874.

The following is a history of his work in this congregation, as is told by Miss Belle Rodgers, in a paper read at the memorial services held after his death:

Eleven years ago, during a vacancy of the pastorate of Henderson congregation, Doctor Wallace consented to preach there for a few months. Henderson had not prospered for some time. The congregation was not very harmonious, and though once a strong and flourishing church, it had been crippled by a series of adverse influences until it was feared disorganization would become a necessity. But in the hour of its extremity, Dr. Wallace expressed a readiness to accept its pastorate. All were pleased, yet surprised at his willingness, with so many discouragements before him. The congregation was small and divided, and the church building old-fashioned and quite uncomfortable in winter. Yet none nor all of these considerations discouraged him, as he felt a strong desire that this mother church should be revived and flourish, and still, by its ministry, gladden many hearts with words of comfort, joy and peace. Another consideration lent additional weight in favor of his acceptance of the pastorate: impaired health made it necessary to devise some plan to aid in its recovery. He thought by a change of labor, even if something additional were imposed, it might afford such relaxation as would prove beneficial. Thus viewing all things, he had a hopeful conviction that this was a work the Lord had given him to do.

After accepting the pastorate in 1873, he was not installed for more than a year—hoping he might the more certainly test his ability to make the relation permanent. After installment, however, he only remained one year before failing health made it impossible for him to do both pastoral and college work. He, therefore, resigned his charge in January, 1876, after having given two and one half years of pastoral labor to the Henderson congregation. As pas-

tor he entered so enthusiastically into the work of the
congregation, when among us, that he and we seemed
to forget he had college duties claiming his attention.
It was his habit, when coming to us, to throw off all
thought of college duties, and enter fully into the work
and spirit of pastoral life; and this, he claimed, was a
relaxation, and constantly asserted its remedial influence, by giving him greater energy and vigor for
college duty.   As soon as he accepted the charge of
the congregation he felt himself the under-shepherd,
and tender, wise oversight was given to all the little
details of pastoral duty, and yet, in each insignifi-
cant place, he dignified his office by evident loyalty
to his Master, the great Teacher.   He was often
seen in the homes of his parishioners, the sick, the
aged, the poor, the irreligious—all received his helpful attention. This was not spasmodic, but was a
constant feature of his work, and many are the tender recollections treasured in the hearts of his parishioners in Henderson for his kind ministrations to
their sick or dying friends.

He soon knew the faces, and learned the names of
each man, woman and child in the congregation, and
as he went among them, on the Sabbath or week day,
greeted each with a smile and word, and vigilantly
noted the absent from church service, and always
made kind inquiries for their welfare. We soon
felt he was interested in our church not only in its
members, but the youth, the children, the poor, and
all the community shared his thoughtful attention.

By his efforts, and at his suggestion, the Sabbath-
school was re-organized, prayer-meetings had greater
interest, while teachers' meetings, woman's mission-

ary society, young peoples' prayer-meeting and
church socials had their beginning there during his
ministry. In his preaching, prayers, and plans of
work in the congregation, the young people had a
large share of his attention. He sought in many
ways to advance their highest interests and best welfare, always devising plans for their religious, moral
and social improvement; at one time giving a course
of lectures calculated to promote this object.

In his preaching, the gospel claims were urgently
pressed, and doctrinal discourse was frequent; and
while popular difficulties were sometimes presented
and answered, yet always remembering the immediate wants of his hearers, presented such truths as
he knew by intercourse with them, might be most
helpful to them.

His pastorate at Henderson might be called eminently successful—not so much in the accessions it
gave to the membership, as by the ability shown in
bringing out latent power. Not that any rare gifts
had lain concealed there more than exists in every
other congregation, but that his tact and enthusiasm
were so infused into the membership, that difficulties there were easily overcome, obstacles were
removed, and mountains made to seem as mole-hills.
And thus it was through these agencies he secured a
friendly, harmonious feeling among the members,
and interested and engaged them in religious work.

While the congregation, being nestled in among
contiguous congregations, increase could only be expected in the ordinary way, and this may doubtless
account for want of larger accessions to the church.

But the time came, all too soon, that his ministrations to us should cease, and with sadness we regretted the necessity for his departure, but still were hopeful that many years might possibly be given him—years of usefulness to the church and the world; but this has been denied us. And now we mourn the loss of a prince in the church; for one has fallen, and, though crowned with many honors, the church had yet another in store for him, to which they were bidding him occupy. The whole church was gladdened at the honors awaiting him, still expecting much golden grain to be reaped by his labors. But at the threshold of the reaping time he is gathered to the harvest home—to the house of his Father. The mourners go about the streets with the windows of the soul darkened, for the golden bowl has been broken, and the spirit has returned to God who gave it.

CHAPTER IV

The work of Dr. Wallace in Monmouth was drawing to a close. He had given to the college his best days. His strength, his energy, his very life was spent in this work. He felt that he was fast breaking down; yet his heart was with the college. It was his Master's work, to which he had consecrated his life; therefore, he could not give it up until he was convinced that he was no longer able to bear the burden. His work, however, as a pastor in Monmouth, was ended. His remaining strength must be devoted to the college. The spiritual interest of the students was upon his heart. He labored with them, and prayed for them, and rejoiced when any gave evidence of the new birth. It was not mere reformation of life, nor only a cultivated and refined scholarship that he sought; but that Christ should be formed in them "the hope of glory."

In his chapel sermons, designed especially for the students, he sought not to display his ability as a metaphysician, or as a mere theologian, nor to exhibit specimens of rhetoric; but he sought to bring what power he possessed to expound and illustrate

(51)

the grand truths of the gospel of the grace of God. and to bring these truths to bear upon the heart and conscience of his hearers, that they might be brought into the full enjoyment of that peace which comes from believing upon the Lord Jesus Christ. While he preached doctrine, and advocated the reforms of the times, both from the pulpit and p.at- form, yet the theme he most delighted to dwell upon was Christ and him crucified. He seemed to enter into these subjects with an earnestness that made his soul glow with divine fervor. When he was called to preach away from home, he generally chose such themes as most fully brought forward "the fulness of the gospel." He seemed to be imbued with the spirit of the words of the Master concern- ing the Apostle to the Gentiles: "He is a chosen vessel unto me, to bear my name before the Gen- tiles, and kings, and the children of Israel." There was no name so precious to him as the name of Jesus, and his desire was to bear this name on every suitable occasion. One who had been a student, and who was intimate with him in later years, says: "His topics away from home were always near the heart of the great idea of human redemption. I re- member some years ago when preaching for him, that he took the opportunity to preach at some half- deserted church, near Wooster. I asked him what he would preach about. 'O,' said he, 'my best

sermon: "Blessed is he whose transgression is forgiven, whose sin is covered." I have no doubt it
was his 'best sermon,' for he was 'best' on such a
subject. ' Sermons,' he said, "are with me the sur-
vival of the fittest,' but we have all noticed that they
were the 'fittest' from having the most spiritual
life."

The doctrines commonly called " the doctrines of
grace" were peculiarly dear to him. On all suitable
occasions, he sought to expound them. An old
acquaintance. Dr. J. T. Cooper, thus writes:

One thing which increased my interest in Dr.
Wallace, was the clearness with which he perceived,
and the tenacity with which he clung to the doctrines of grace, as they are set forth in the famous
work entitled, " The Marrow of Modern Divinity,"
and in the writings of Thomas Boston, and the
Erskines. and the late Dr. John Anderson, particularly in his work entitled " Saving Faith." As is
well known to his immediate friends, he was brought
to embrace these views as the only views
which are strictly deserving the name of gospel truth, and as the only views that can
bring a true and settled peace to the conscience.
I was but a short time acquainted with this brother,
before I was brought to a discovery of his mind in
relation to these matters, and I need not conceal the
fact that it formed a sacred bond of friendship and
fellowship between him and the writer. I may also
be permitted to remark that. in my judgment, the
strong sympathy which the Doctor cherished for

these "Marrow Doctrines," and the great importance
which he attached to them, imparted to his sermons
a richness and unction, which the spiritually minded
could hardly fail to appreciate.

His decision to leave the college was reached by
a slow and painful process. Years before he had
solemnly consecrated himself to the cause of Christian education in Monmouth College. For this he
labored, sacrificing both comfort and pecuniary
profits. But he could not leave this work until it
was plain that his Master so decreed. The manner
in which he came to this conclusion will be best seen
from extracts from his diary; these will show the
care that was taken as well as the mental process
passed through in coming to this conclusion:

On Monday, February 7, 1876, I placed my resignation as President of Monmouth College in the
hands of the Trustees, because I was no longer competent to perform the duties of the office. The
Trustees tendered me six months' vacation, in case I
should withdraw my resignation. I did so on condition that I should be at liberty to renew it at Commencement. This was accepted.

The greater part of this vacation was spent at Fall
River, Mass., in order to get the benefit of the sea
air. Concerning the time spent there, he thus
writes:

I selected the following subjects for prayer: 1.
Restoration to health. 2. Guidance. 3. Abiding

peace. 4. Holiness. 5. Spirit of power. 6. Supply of my need. 7. Family. 8. College. 9. Cause of Christ. For these things I have been daily praying, and now on this, the sixteenth day of June, 1876—my fifty-first birthday—I am able to record: 1. That my health has greatly improved, so that I feel competent once more for duty. 2. I think I have been guided by God; to-day the way seems clear. God placed me at Monmouth; the reasons that have led me to resign have been removed; there is no cause why I should not return; as far as I can see, my mind is clear. 3. I have enjoyed abiding peace. 4. My wants have been supplied; when I have had little, there has been no lack; much, there has been nothing over. 5. I have been enabled, as far as I can see, to walk worthy in some good degree of my profession. 6. My family give me no trouble and but little anxiety. 7. The college has been conducted prosperously during my absence. It now seems to me to be my duty to do all I can, while here, to improve my health; at the appointed time to return to Monmouth and devote myself to the promotion of the cause of Christ in connection with the college. The time now is short, and it becomes me to mass my forces and seek to do effectually the work that has been assigned me—*the work of Christian Education in Monmouth College;* and my prayer is that my latter days may be blessed more, much more, than my beginning.

He returned to the duties of his office at the beginning of the college year in 1876, and continued without any serious interruption until the Com-

mencement of the college year in 1877. His diary
continues:

A week after, my power of work and endurance
gave way. Quit preaching in Chapel and everything I could. Had a couple of weeks' vacation. In
November came a unanimous call from Wooster,
Ohio, and. soon after, notice of election to Chicago.
College Trustees raised my salary $700 to enable
me to take my vacation and rest. And now, what
shall I do? I have been trusting and praying for
guidance. To-day, December 8, seeking it formally
and specially.

Shall I leave the college or remain? I. The facts
in favor of remaining: 1. I am in the college; presumption is in favor of remaining. 2. My salary
has been made abundant. 3. Faculty, students,
trustees, everybody seems to favor my remaining.
4. I understand college work and have been prospered in it. 5. There is here a wide and very important field of usefulness, never more important. 6.
There is danger, that in case I leave, the college will
suffer serious hurt. 7. I am here among my family
and my friends, who have tried and trusted me. 8.
Almost all my reputation, knowledge and skill, acquired here as President of the College, would be
lost capital.

II. Facts adverse. 1. My health is such as to
disqualify me for duty. I have not been able for
anything like full work, for three months: and that,
too, while my duty is not heavy; or nearly as heavy
as it once was. No heavier than the President of
the college ought to perform. 2. During last year,

after the rest of four months, I could hardly perform duty, and broke down under vacation and opening work. 3. This is the third time I have given out: First, in February, 1875, continued until Commencement, when I was prevented from resigning by physicians and faculty. Second, in January, 1876, or rather early in previous term. Resigned in February, and withdrew on promise of rest. 4. For nearly three years, except last year, I have been unable to push college work as it demands. 5. If I remain here I shall be unable to do anything but the most necessary college work—oversee, teach and preach— ut little lecturing abroad, but little writing. 6. I shall be constantly subject to ill turns, and in danger of finally and completely breaking down. 7. Called to the pastorate in 1872, in Allegheny; declined. To the pastorate in 1874, in St. Louis; declined. Since that time, excepting last year, been disabled. Called again; does it not look as if it was the Lord's mind that I should return to it? 8. Remaining in the college, I am in imminent danger of disappointing its friends, and being unable to do what is expected of me, and becoming a burden to it, rather than being a help. 9. The college is not able to increase my salary—danger of mischief from it. 10. Fields of great usefulness, with much less work and less responsibilities are open for me. in which I shall have a much better opportunity of doing much needed work, which I can not do here. 11. The faculty can run the college until a new president is found. 12. I have reason to believe that my health would be better in another climate, or from a change.

Continued calling and crying for light until the 18th. It now appears thus: 1. No man ought to accept or continue to hold a place, the duties of which he is not able to discharge. Reliable health needed in president. I have not been able to perform the duties of my office for two years out of the last three. I see no prospect of being able in the future, judging from the past. Very heavy work is now demanded of the president. 2. I have opened to me now a position of great usefulness, the duties of which I can adequately discharge. 3. The risks from remaining seem to me much greater than from my going: (1). The less I am in college and the less fully I perform the duties of my position, the less my influence and the lower my standing; the less my value to the college; the more difficult to raise my salary. (2). The danger of completely breaking down, and becoming a burden to the college and my friends. (3). The danger of discontent and dissatisfaction from my salary being made so high. (4). The risks to the college from my leaving slight. 4. If I remain, the strength of my declining years will be given to more secular work: if I go, to more spiritual. 5. I have no reason to believe that my health can be depended upon to be adequate to enable me to perform the duties of the college, as I think they ought to be performed. as I would feel in conscience bound to perform them. It is not *reliable*. 6. The prompt, decided. spontaneous judgments of several men, my friends and intimate acquaintances, are, that I ought to leave the college; among them Drs. Mathews, J. Brown, and Hamilton. 7. My leaving will facilitate the only correct policy for college: economize, collect, pay debts, and elect a president after first six months.

My health is not reliable enough to justify me continuing in the college. I love it too well and judge its interests too important to remain with it.

On Monday evening, December 17, 1 went into my room in college, intending to remain until light came. I fell on my knees in prayer. Then came to my mind these words: "Not to-night, but in the morning." I accepted it as from God. I at once went home, and the next morning went to my study and sought to know the Lord's mind. While in prayer, my mind settled down in this conviction, that I ought not to hold a position of which I could not perform the duties. I arose and went over the considerations pro and con. Again I sought light; again my mind settled down in the same conviction. I then went over and talked with Bro. Ure. I asked him if he had any thing additional to say. He said not; but remarked. that I ought not to remain, if I felt my health was too unreliable to perform college work. I went home again and again threw myself on my knees, and besought the Lord to show me His will, let it be what it might. Again my mind settled down in the conviction that my health was too unreliable to justify me in continuing in the presidency. I sought the Lord for some token from Him that this was His mind—that I was right and not deceived. I then went up to my room, when there came on a feeling of faintness, which I accepted as a "*sign from God*" that I was too nearly worn out to continue in such an important position.

That evening I called the faculty and announced my decision. The next morning I sent in my resignation to the trustees—there was a full meeting. J. G. Madden moved that my resignation be accepted, Dr. Matthews seconded the motion, remarking that I could do nothing else. It was accepted to take effect, January 1, 1878, and my salary continued until June. That day I announced the result to the students. I was much prostrated the rest of the week.

In 1856, Dr. Wallace came to Monmouth to take charge of the young college. January 1, 1878, after twenty-one years, he laid down the work, with what measure of success has been told in a previous chapter. He came to Monmouth strong and robust; he left it a wreck. It may be truly said, that he sacrificed himself for the cause of Christian education in Monmouth College. He ceased from this work only because he was unable to prosecute it further. Other positions, far easier, and much more lucrative, were tendered to him but he could not accept them; for he had consecrated himself to this work and he dare not lay it aside. He had put his hand to the plow, as he felt, at the call of the Master, and without that Master's command he could not let go. The days following the commencement of the work at Monmouth were dark. The political horizon was dark; the financial condition of the country was deplorable. To start, equip and endow a college, required herculean efforts, and great self-denial. While others stood by to aid, yet the burden fell upon his shoulders. He faltered not, but stood under the burden until it was manifestly impossible for him to longer endure the strain.

Another has said: "It was his one remark to me, in speaking of his leaving the college, that it did not seem to be the Master's will that any one person should begin and carry on to completion any great work. The law of the kingdom has always been, 'one soweth and the other reapeth.' To Dr. Wallace, it seemed to be given in many things to preside over beginnings. His hands laid the foundation; others reared the superstructure. He sowed the seed and others reaped the harvest of his toil, as coming generations will reap the fruit of their labor."

CHAPTER V.

The different positions held by Dr. Wallace, or tendered him, came unsought, very frequently in the face of decided protest. Yet, when a position was offered to him, he always gave it a careful consideraton. His one desire seemed to be to know the mind of the Lord in the matter. He was very slow in concluding to leave one place of labor for another. He felt that if the Master gave him a field to occupy, he must remain until his work was completed. The advice he gave to others—and it was the one he himself always followed—was, "The Master has placed you where you now are, and the presumption is in favor of your remaining. If you change, there must be good and sufficient reasons for so doing." The consciousness of doing his Master's will became a force which carried him over very many difficulties.

In October of 1877, being in Ohio, he was constrained to visit Wooster, and preach one Sabbath. This was before he had decided that he must give up college work. He consented to go to Wooster only with the express understanding that he was not to be considered in any sense a candidate. However,

(62)

the result was a unanimous call to him to become pastor of that congregation. About the same time another call was extended to him by the United Presbyterian Congregation of Chicago. His decision in reference to these is thus told in his diary, the entry being dated at Wooster:

I decided not to go to Chicago, because it appeared to me that the work and responsibility there would be so heavy as to give me but little relief. All my physicians and friends united in the conviction that it would be folly for me to go to a place where the life would be so intense as there. My mind was inclined to Wooster, because: (1.) It seemed to me quite an easy place, comparatively, and not beyond my strength. (2.) The call from there was unexpected. unsought and spontaneous, hearty, unanimous, and what might be called providential. (3.) Seeking constantly to know my Master's mind, it seemed to me His will that I should come here.

He left Monmouth December 27, and reached Wooster the next evening. His convictions after arriving in Wooster are thus given: "I am at rest. A clear inspection of the field satisfies me that it will suit me well. I can rest and study as I could not have done elsewhere. I thank God for doing so much for me. I have enjoyed great peace since I decided the question. The experiment I have made of my God, as a covenant-keeping God, has strengthened my faith and filled me with unutterable gladness. The fortieth Psalm, first verses, have expressed my feelings."

The following, as subjects of daily prayer, are taken from entries made while engaged in the pastoral work at Wooster:

1. That the Lord would show me day by day what I ought to do. 2. That He would strengthen me for all duty. 3. That He would show me a suitable house. 4. That He would bless the congregation in all things, and my work in it. 5. That He would bless my wife and children. 6. That He would bless Monmouth College, and give it a President. 7. That He would make it apparent to my friends and the church that He had guided me in bringing me here; that I had not done wrong, but right in coming.

Following this table of prayer topics in this line of comment and date: "All the above answered to the letter. Jan. 8, 1880."

For the first six months after he began his labors in Wooster, he was able to do but very little severe mental work. He spent his time in visiting the members of the congregation and re-organizing the congregation for Christian work. Difficulties that had arisen previous to his settlement there were to be settled—members were to be reconciled; all this was happily effected. During his college years his preaching had often, on account of other pressing duties, to be done without adequate preparation. This he greatly regretted, but, in Wooster, after his health began to improve, he was able to give much more time to pulpit preparation. The labor he was able to perform here was by carefully systematizing his work. He endeavored always to have a subject for the coming Sabbath, selected the week previous, never later than Monday. Thus he was able to commence the study of his subject the first thing on Tuesday morning, if desired.

He frequently preached series of discourses. He lectured upon the book of Revelation throughout. He gave a course of Sabbath evening lectures upon the commandments. These were listened to by full houses. He also gave a course of lectures upon the "Distinctive Principles" of his church. The discourse upon "secret societies" was listened to by many who were themselves members of these societies. While he endeavored to present his objections to such societies in a clear and forcible manner, yet he did so in such a way as not to antagonize individuals. He was respected and listened to by those who differed from him upon these things. About once a month he gave a lecture designed especially for the young people. About once every quarter he preached a sermon for the children.

Although his health improved after coming to Wooster, yet he never was well. Dr. Taggart, who was his physician there, says: "It is well known that Dr. Wallace came to Wooster an invalid—a

5

wreck. His nervous system was much exhausted from over work. There were times when he felt his old ability to work for the Master; yet there were many times, and some of them protracted, in which he was not able to do much work. The great secret lay in the exhaustion of the nerve center. He would have a sense of constriction, and an apparent diffi- culty in breathing, so that in walking he would have to stop and stand still a few minutes to rest. I could find no organic disease of the heart, and no disease of the lungs—nothing of that kind that would account for the trouble, and I referred the matter to nervous exhaustion—exhaustion of the nerve center that presided over respiration and breathing." Thus all the labor he performed was under great bodily affliction. In August, 1881, after a year of hard work he was prostrated with gastralgia, or neuralgia of the stomach. He was unable to do any work until about the first of Octo- ber. In January, he was again prostrated. He was unable to return to his work until March, and then able only to do a limited amount. About the last of May, he had another severe attack. The congregation gave him a vacation for four months. This he spent at Clifton Springs, N. Y., and Ocean Grove, N. J.

During his stay at these places he had much time at his disposal. This time was not spent in idleness. It was not in his nature to be idle. He always felt that the Master had a work for him to do, and it was his object to be prepared for doing that work. He felt the time for work was very uncertain, and this led him to a renewed act of consecration. This "act" we find in his diary, and we here give it:

Before I return to my work, I do to-day, solemnly, and in the presence of God, give myself to Him, body and soul, wholly and without reserve: I give myself up to Him to make of me what He would have me to be; to put me in the position He would have me occupy; to bear whatever burdens He would lay upon me; to do the work He may appoint me; and to enjoy whatever measure of blessings He may grant me. My heart's desire is that God would accept this gift and seal me as His own, fill me with His spirit, make me holy, fit me for His service, lead and guide me, strengthen and sustain me. I do take God in Christ to be my God and Father; Jesus to be my Saviour, my Prophet, my Priest, my King: the Holy Spirit to be my Comforter and Sanctifier; I trust and look to God to treat me as a child, granting me all the rights and privileges of a child; and submit to Him as a child to a father. I trust and look to Jesus as my Prophet, to teach me all that I need to know, and submit to Him as my Prophet; I look to, trust in, and submit to Him as my Priest, to obtain for me all the blessings I need; I look to Him and trust in Him as my King, to subdue me to Himself, to reign in me, to rule over me, and to restrain and conquer His and my enemies. I trust

in, look too, and submit to the Holy Spirit as my
helper in all things. "I believe; Lord help my
unbelief."

From his diary we find that he spent much of his
time in the study of the Word of God, and in reading devotional books; in meditation and in prayer;
prayer that he might be "filled with the Spirit; that
all that is meant by the baptism of the Spirit, the
leading of the Spirit, the witness of the Spirit might
be his;" that he "might be led by the Spirit, guided
by the Spirit, and live in the Spirit;" and
"that he might be kept from grieving Him."
But his prayer was not for himself alone;
others were remembered—his family, his congregation and the church at large, that God
would pour out his Spirit upon the church. He returned to his home Sept. 10 much improved, both
in body and in spirit.

The Board of Managers of Xenia Theological
Seminary at their meeting in the spring of 1882,
selected Drs. French and Wallace "to deliver a
series of seven lectures each on Apologetics, and
more particularly on the Evidences of Christianity."
The main design was to supplement the work of the
corps of teachers, which by the death of Dr. Bruce
had been reduced to three. "Their work was divided
between them thus: Dr. French lectured on the
external evidences of Christianity, Dr. Wallace on

the internal. The latter's work lay chiefly, if not
entirely, in directing the attention of the class to the
proofs of the Divine origin and authority of the
Bible as found in the sacred volume itself. Nevertheless he took a somewhat wider survey of the subject, and introduced much of his own experience, the
results of a long and very active life, as a teacher
and minister of the Word, thus giving the students
the benefit of a large acquaintance with men and
books." "I heard portions of several of his lectures,
and more than once he would start from his chair in
the delivery, get to his feet and pour out a stream
of impassioned eloquence, which one does not hear
often in the class room? He created much enthusiasm in the seminary by these lectures, he was very
stimulating in all his work, and the benefits result-
ing therefrom lasted through the rest of the session."

At the meeting of the Board of Managers in
March, 1883, he was nominated to the synods having control of the seminary, for a professorship. The
synods at their meetings in the fall elected him to
this position. After careful consideration he had
decided to accept and was preparing to move to
Xenia, to enter upon this work; but his Master called
him home.

In June of 1883, the Board of Trustees of West-
minster College, New Wilmington, Pennsylvania,
elected him to the office of president. This position,

after careful consideration, he felt it his duty to decline. He felt that the work which would be required of the president of that institution, would be entirely beyond what his failing health would warrant him in undertaking.

He was appointed by the presbytery of Mansfield, a delegate to the General Assembly which met in Pittsburgh, May 23, 1883. The question of the use of "Instruments in the worship of God" came before this Assembly. It had been decided by the previous Assembly, that the law forbidding the use of instruments had been repealed. Those opposed to the use of instruments felt themselves aggrieved, and asked that this Assembly "declare 'explicitly that in none of the congregations under the care of the Assembly can instrumental music be lawfully used in worship until the church shall have decided by constitutional enactment that such music in worship is divinely authorized and prescribed." It is not our intention to speak of this discussion, only to state the position of Dr. Wallace upon this question. When the rule was adopted in 1867, he, with one other member of the presbytery, neither voted for nor against it, "believing that the use of instruments was inexpedient, but not forbidden by the Word of God." When the subject came up in overture in 1881, he, with others voted to repeal the rule. There was no change in his convictions, only he deemed it inexpedient to have any rule upon the subject. The Assembly of 1883 passed the following resolution: "That Drs. Joseph T. Cooper. David A. Wallace and James P. Lytle be appointed a committee to address a pastoral letter to our people. setting forth the true state of the question as settled by the church, and urging upon them the respect due the authority of the church and to each other as Christian brethren."

Dr. Cooper, as chairman of the committee, prepared the "letter," and submitted it to Dr. Wallace, who with but few suggestions approved as prepared, and this, together with one from Dr. Lytle, was sent forth to the church on its errand of peace. Dr. Cooper thus writes: "We had much conversation in relation to this controversy that has to such a degree so painfully agitated our beloved church. We both deplored the introduction of the question in view of the sad separations which it had made among brethren. We were both, however, fully agreed that it was one of those things which in the light of Scripture and reason may be regarded as legitimate subjects of forbearance and that the controversy never could be settled on any other basis."

The twelve months intervening between the adjournment of the Assembly of 1882, and the convening of the Assembly of 1883. were months of painful anxiety to many who loved the church of their choice. The question that was frequently asked was, "What will be the result? will there be a division?" Dr. Wallace was no idle spectator of what was passing. He loved the United Presbyterian Church; it was the church of his birth, and of his choice. He could not be unconcerned, when her unity, if not her very existence, was threatened.

One who was with him that summer at Clifton Springs and Ocean Grove gives the following:

We were intimate companions boarding in the same house, occupying adjoining rooms, and hence were much in conversation, and always enjoyed our morning and evening devotions together. The burden of his plans and prayers was an amicable adjustment of the difficulties which threatened to disrupt the church, and alienate brethren who had hitherto "taken sweet counsel together" in the work of the Lord. I could not fail to mark the tenderness and earnestness of his petitions for "the peace of our beloved Zion." Dr. Wallace had his own well-defined opinions as to the merits of the question in dispute, as also of the decisions of the Assembly of 1882. It was not because he did not have clearly defined convictions of his own, but because his ardent love for his church was supreme, that he was able to suppress his own personal preferences, and plead with God and his brethren for such a compromise of their opinions as would be at once consistent, and reconcile differences, restore confidence, and secure harmony in faith, work and worship.

Immediately on his arrival at Clifton Springs, he opened a correspondence with leading brethren on the opposite sides. My knowledge of that corres-

pondence warrants me in stating that it was prompted by the hope of securing such a reconciliation as
would secure the perpetuity of the United Presbyterian Church in her organic unity; and it was inspired by pure and unselfish love for the denomination whose banner he had so long supported.
Those to whom he addressed his communications
failed, in part, to drink in his spirit of reconciliation,
or consent to the measures he proposed. Disappointed, discouraged, yet hopeful, he remarked to
me one day: "I will try once more." He went to
his room wearing a look of deep solicitude, and, after
hours of painful thought—and, may we not conjec-
ture, earnest prayer?—he came to my room to read
to me the message he had indited. His very soul
seemed on fire as he began to read. As he proceeded, the emotions that struggled in his bosom
were with difficulty suppressed. At first, his great
heart seemed to burst as he read in broken, choking
accents: "Can't something be done to save the
United Presbyterian church; the church of my birth
and love; the church to which I have given the
energies of my life; the church by which I have
stood when greater emoluments than she could give
were offering; the church in which I shall live and
die?" Having reached this point, his pent-up tears,
the indices of a struggling soul within, burst forth,
and his very frame shook with emotions, as that
grand hero of many a well-fought battle sat and
sobbed and wept copious, scalding tears over the
church of his love and choice. Whatever the effect
of these communications may have been, it was written by an honest hand, indited by a master mind,

and inspired by a love of his denomination, which challenges the emulation of those whom he has left behind.

In the fall of the year 1883, having decided to accept the position to which he had been elected in the Theological Seminary, he was preparing to remove to Xenia, in order to engage in this work. In the meantime, however, in the State election that was to occur on October 9, an important question was before the people—one that enlisted the sympathies and aroused the energies of Dr. Wallace. The question of amending the constitution of the State, so as to prohibit the manufacture and sale of intoxicating liquors was to be voted at that election. The friends of the measure were doing all in their power to arose public sentiment upon the question. Dr. Wallace was invited to deliver a lecture on the subject at a place twelve miles from Wooster. He spoke to a large audience with his usual force and earnestness. He returned home with the symptoms of having contracted a severe cold. This continued for a few days, but had measurably abated. On the following Sabbath communion services were held in the congregation. He was able to address only a few remarks to the people on Sabbath. All the other services were conducted by Rev. J. M. Farrar, who was assisting him on that occasion. This was the last time he was permitted to be present in the public worship of God.

An account of the closing days of his life, we condense from remarks made by Dr. Taggart, at the funeral services held in Monmouth:

In a day or two there was developed the characteristic symptoms of spasmodic asthma, which grew worse. He did not suffer excruciating pain, but suffered the agony of a man who was struggling to obtain breath, or to get air into his lungs. He had to sit in his chair for over a week without going to bed, as immediately after he would lie down this difficult spasmodic respiration would commence. Other physicians were called, who concurred in the diagnoses which had been made. This difficulty continued in spite of all remedies until the Friday before his death. On Saturday he seemed very much better. He remained in bed all Saturday night and obtained considerable rest. I went to see him on Sabbath morning, and asked him whether preaching should be announced for next Sabbath. "Yes," said he. "announce preaching, and if I am not able to preach, I will make arrangements." In the evening I went to see him again. I found him lying in bed; he was able to lie without any difficulty in breathing. I gave the necessary directions, bade him good evening, and he bade me good evening. He spoke in an ordinary tone of voice, without apparent difficulty. About ten o'clock that night I was called up to go and see him. I learned on my arrival that about half-past nine o'clock, he thought he could go to sleep, and asked for a few drops of chloroform, and thought if he had this he could go asleep. After some hesitation on the part of his wife, it was given to him from a handkerchief. He turned over as if going asleep, and his wife passed into another room. He was alone, the rest of the family having retired. After remaining in an adjoining room for a few minutes, she heard a coughing or sneezing. She went to him; he had turned over on his back, and immediately gave one or two short gasps, and all was over. He slept well that night—he slept in peace. He fell asleep on Sabbath, October 21, 1883, at ten o'clock P. M.

He was well aware of his uncertain condition; he had given directions in reference to certain things in case of his death, but no special preparation was necessary. His work on earth was completed; the Master, whose he was and whom he served, called him home to himself.

Funeral services were held at Wooster. By his request his former colleague, Dr. Alexander Young, preached the sermon. His remains were taken to Monmouth, and, after suitable services in the College Chapel, they were borne to their last resting-place. On Sabbath afternoon, October 28, "Memorial Services" were held in the Opera House, attended by a large concourse of people.

Of his immediate family, a wife, who had been his faithful companion and helper during his busy life; one who had counseled him in times of difficulty, and rejoiced with him in times of prosperity, and cared and watched over him in times of sickness, lives to mourn her loss. Four sons and one daughter remain deprived of a father's counsel.

We close this imperfect sketch of a busy life; a life consecrated to the Lord Jesus; a life of self-denying labor on behalf of others. These labors cannot be told by any pen; these tears which were shed; the anxious hours that were spent, have a voice, but they speak not a language that can be written.

> "Faithful to death. O man of God, well done!
> Thy fight is ended; thy crown is won!"

PART SECOND

DEAD, YET SPEAKING.

(79)

CLAIMS OF THE BIBLE.

Inaugural Address delivered at Monmouth, Ill., Sept. 1, 1857.

Education is the subject of almost universal attention. But few themes are, at the present time, more generally or earnestly discussed. The popular mind is awake to its importance, deeply interested in promoting it. To secure general and thorough mental culture, much money is expended, great efforts are put forth. This is true in the West as well as in the East; in Illinois no less than in Massachusetts.

We are here founding an institution for the promotion of education in its higher departments. And now, at the outset, when our measures are receiving shape and character, it is all-important that the ends proposed, and methods to be employed in such an institution should be well understood. This whole subject we should all carefully consider.

This theme, appropriate as it is to the occasion, I cannot now fully discuss. I must very much narrow my range of thought, or very much transgress the limits assigned me.

In unfolding " The Claims of the Bible to a place as a text book in the College Curriculum," I shall

6   (81)

bring to view the great principles which most pressingly demand attention.

Elsewhere, and at another time, it might have been necessary, at the outset, to have introduced such considerations as would ward off prejudice and secure an unimpassioned hearing. Surely, however, it is not necessary here or at this time of day that a moment should be thus occupied. My aim is to show that the Bible ought to have a place in the course of study of every Collegiate Institution—that the Bible in its original languages, its history, its philosophy, its theology, ought to be studied as carefully and thoroughly, and recited as regularly and faithfully as any text-book in any department of Literature or Science.

With the view of illustrating and confirming this position, I invite your attention to the ends of education and the methods by which they are secured.

And what is the end of education? To qualify for the more successful acquisition of material wealth? Of a widely extended and brilliant reputation? for grasping and wielding successfully the sceptre of power? for deriving more exquisite enjoyment from sensual pleasures? surely none of these things. Surely no material good constitutes the great end of education.

What then is it? · I answer without hesitation: The great ultimate end of education is to fit man for accomplishing, to some good degree, the end of his being.

Again the inquiry arises, " What is the chief end of man? " The answer to this question has been settled for at least two hundred years: " Man's chief end is to glorify God and enjoy him forever. " I shall attempt no elaborate exposition of this definition. All, however, will at once acknowledge that man most effectually accomplishes the great end of his being, most fully glorifies God and enjoys him, when he is most completely obedient in heart and life to that law which enjoins love to God and love to man, when he is most nearly conformed to God in his moral character, and when being qualified therefor, he accomplishes the most in advancing the highest well-being of his fellow-men. In just so far as a man is eminently good and mighty in doing good, in so far does he accomplish the chief end of his being.

All true education contemplates these ultimate ends and is adapted to secure them.

Its special objects subordinate to this great end are—

1. The communication of useful knowledge.

2. The culture of the intellectual powers.

3. The formation of an elevated moral character.

Any process of education that gains these ends to any good degree, so far qualifies its subject for accomplishing the great end of his being.

Let us now examine these special ends that we may ascertain how far the use of the Bible, as a text-book, will contribute, or is necessary to secure them.

The first is: The communication of knowledge. The great design of the knowledge communicated in a course of academic instruction is to prepare for the study of a profession, and to qualify for a proper discharge of the ordinary duties of life. No profession can be successfully studied without at least some previous knowledge of the great principles of literature and science. Hence, those who aim at a full and complete equipment for entering on this department of intellectual effort are led through a course of instruction in Latin, Greek, the various subjects of mathematics, and of natural, moral and mental philosophy. Thus furnished, progress in professional study, otherwise slow and toilsome, becomes easy and rapid.

Knowledge is necessary to the most successful discharge of the duties of life. A man entirely ignorant of the subjects of the college course may live a happy and useful life; certainly, however, such an increase of knowledge as the study of these subjects secures, would render that life much more useful. And it must be conceded on all hands that ignorance here is absolutely incompatible with any very successful discharge of the ordinary duties of life.

A knowledge of the principles of literature and science is then important. There is, however, a knowledge much more important—a knowledge essential to an upright, happy and useful life. He that lives such a life, be it professional or non-professional, public or private, must know what is right and what is wrong, and how to distinguish the one from the other; he must know how he may be reconciled to an offended God, and live at peace with him; and how he may be freed from every unholy affection and come to cherish those elevated sentiments that assimilate the human to the divine; he must know those magnificent truths, from whose unfathomable depths alone can be drawn motives adequate to raise men from the dust, and constrain them to enter the elevated walks of true obedience to the great lawgiver; and, if in his whole career, he does aught for his fellow man, he must understand well those eternal principles in accordance with which alone man's most momentous interests can be successfully promoted. He that lives a life worthy of a man—a life that will at all answer the demands of the end of his being—must know all this. It is absolutely indispensible.

Now, where shall this knowledge be found? Certainly not in the speculations of Plato or Aristotle; certainly not in the ethics of Cicero or Seneca. The brightest genius that ever soared through the boundless fields of immensity, baffled, disappointed, humbled in his vain attempts to find out this wisdom, is compelled to confess: "Such knowledge is too wonderful for me; it is high; I can not attain unto it." We must go and sit at the feet of him who spake as never man spake, and learn from the simple, yet sublime words that fell from his lips. We must find this knowledge, so necessary, in the "Word of Christ." If, then, that instruction, essential to qualify man for accomplishing, to any good degree, the end of his being, is given at all our colleges, the Bible must be our text book.

I have said that the knowledge derived from the study of the Word of God is more important than that derived from the study of all the other subjects granted a place in the College course. Contrast the two. From the one the student becomes familiar with the grand old tongues of the Greeks and Romans, incorporated so intimately with our own manly, vigorous Anglo-Saxon, the depositories of inexhaustible stores of valuable knowledge, of the antiquities, the history, the poetry, the philosophy of those renowned peoples; he becomes familiar with the principles of mathematical science, so important in actual life; with the art of vigorous, impressive, elegant utterance; with the elements of science, natural, mental, political, and moral; nor is his work complete until he has surveyed the Evidences of

Christianity, learned what of religion he may from nature, and examined the analogies of the natural to the revealed. The faithful student, in the usual course of study, becomes familiar with this varied and confessedly important knowledge. Here, however, he ordinarily stops. Bible truth is rarely granted a place among these subjects. But, let us view for a moment, the knowledge that may be derived from this study. Here, at the outset, he learns a language surely not less worthy of being known than any other—the depository of learning—of antiquities, history, poetry, philosophy—surely not less interesting and important than those of Greece and Rome. As he proceeds he learns certain knowledge of truth, in relation to which "he might dig with toilsome and painful efforts, in the mines of Pagan literature for many long years, without one ray of light shining upon him in these dreary caverns." He learns the being and attributes of the Supreme Jehovah, the Creator and Governor of all; the origin of sin—the disease that infects us all—its nature, its infinite baseness, its eternally ruinous consequences; the way of deliverance from its power and penalty; a pure and heavenly morality, the realization of which, in heart and life, assimilates man to his God. And all through its sacred pages are scattered motives to the noblest life man can live, drawn from the depths of hell, the heights of heaven, the remotest eternity. In the former, the student is led up the gorgeous avenues that lead to the temple of Divine truth; he is bidden walk round about it; he is shown its foundations, deep and solid, of massive granite; its pillars of polished marble: its beautiful proportions and lofty turrets. Perhaps he is permitted to stop a moment at the threshold, glance within, and catch a glimpse of the magnificence treasured there. In the latter he is led through its halls, along its corridors, bidden repose in its alcoves, at every step shown the beauty and glory that adorn it, and taught to bow in homage before the God who manifests his presence there. Is not this much the more desirable? I submit it to the calm judgment of any clear-headed and honest-hearted man, does not this knowledge excel in importance the knowledge of the whole range of literature and science found in the most extended College curriculum, by a measure whose length from first to last is infinity? A man may dispense with the former, but it is only at a price no man can afford to pay that he neglects the latter. Are the claims of the subjects usually granted a place in the course of study strong? Then I ask, are not the claims of Biblical literature and science a thousand-fold stronger?

2. Another special end of education is the culture of the intellectual powers.

This end is altogether distinct from the communi-

cation of knowledge. It is also, altogether more
important. And here multitudes are radically mistaken. According to a view by far too common,
education is simply teaching. The mind is a huge
storehouse; the filling up thereof with various
knowledge is the great business of education. He
who in the shortest period, deposits here the largest
mass of facts is the best educator. He who gathers
knowledge most rapidly is the best student. On
this theory much of the popular education is conducted. Such a process, however, scarce deserves
the name of education. The most successful teacher
in a common sense of the term, is often a most contemptible charlatan. Under such a process, a student can very speedily be crammed with what is called
learning, and at the same time be totally destitute
of power to use his acquisitions to any important
purpose. The reason is found in the simple fact,
that notwithstanding all his acquisitions, his higher
faculties remain undeveloped. He has gained no
power.

That education which is successful only in communicating knowledge, accomplishes only a secondary and comparatively unimportant work. A higher
and much more important end is intellectual culture.

The human intellect is a unit possessed of various powers. These as arranged and classified by

President Wayland, are Perception, Consciousness, Original Suggestion, Abstraction, Memory, Reason, Imagination and Taste. To develop these faculties is the great object of education, so far as it is merely intellectual. To cultivate these faculties, to train the mind to perceive accurately and promptly the qualities of things around, to discern accurately and promptly its own varying state; to follow out successfully those endless chains of thought bound together by the laws of association, to concentrate itself on a single subject or a single quality until fully examined and thoroughly understood, to trace resemblances, to detect diversities, to group individuals into species, species into genera, to rise from particulars to generals, until the great principles of truth are fully eliminated and firmly grasped; to treasure facts rapidly, retain them firmly, and recall them promptly and correctly; to form right judgments, to draw sound conclusions, to rise from the known to the unknown, and thus starting with the facts of perception and consciousness to advance onward boldly and confidently into the realms of the unexplored and determine what there is true, to group into one image conceptions widely diverse, and thus form pictures of utility, beauty, grandeur, and sublimity before unknown, to delight in the truly beautiful, in the natural, moral and spiritual worlds, and turn displeased from the opposite; to subordi-

nate all the faculties to the stern-authority of the
will, to express accurately, earnestly, impressively
its varied thoughts and feelings, as to enable the
man to instruct, to convince, to persuade, to arouse
his fellows—in a word, to control them at his pleasure—these are the ends legitimately contemplated in
intellectual training;—Accomplishing these, it accomplishes its proper object.

With the man trained thus, it is easy work to
acquire knowledge. Master of his own powers, able
to use them at his pleasure, he grasps without difficulty the facts and principles of every department
of learning; with giant strides, he stalks through
the fields of professional study, outstripping every
untrained competitor; at a sitting, he masters the
most abstruse discussions; a few hours suffice to
put him in possession of the most intricate science;
the facts of history he makes his own, one would
think by intuition. No subject is hidden from him;
in his hand is the key that unlocks the storehouse
of knowledge. In the process of training, he
acquires knowledge of vast service in his future
career; yet, until the disciplinary process has done
its work, until he is master of his powers, and has
learned to subordinate them to his purpose. he is not
prepared for the proper work of acquisition. no more
than the mechanic is prepared to execute the deli-
cate process of his art, until he has been trained to

the skillful use of his instruments. Education precedes learning.

To all it must be apparent that the man thus educated is mighty—a giant among men. With his tongue or with his pen. he wields a controlling influence. Men bow before him and do him homage. As he narrates his facts, deduces his principles, portrays the creations of his imagination, exhibits his pictures, men yield themselves to his control, glow with admiration, tremble with passion, burn with indignation, melt with sympathy, rush to action, at his pleasure.

This education is not the work of a day. It is no. child's play. When years of patient, severe, wearisome toil have been expended, the work, in many instances, is still very inadequately accomplished. Yet he who would grasp the sceptre and wield it, who would be a king among men, must submit to just this long, toilsome process. It is the great business of education, so far as it is intellectual, to secure this culture. It fails essentially, if it fails here; if successful here, it does not come far short anywhere.

With a view of affording this culture, every intelligent system of education is arranged. The ancient languages, the various subjects of pure mathematics, philosophy, natural, mental, political, and moral, occupy a place in every College course, because the almost universal testimony of educators, for centuries, witnesses that the study of these subjects is eminently adapted to furnish this culture. Now, I claim for the literature and science of the Bible, a place in this curriculum. I am bound to point out their qualifications for this position.

Will the student find any higher culture in the study of Latin, than in the study of Hebrew? In the study of the annals of our world as recorded by the historians of Greece and Rome, of Europe and America, than in the study of those annals recorded by the historians of Israel and Judah? In the study of the Greek and Roman, of the Italian, German and English poets, than in the study of the more pathetic, more stirring, more sublime and infinitely purer poetry of Judea? Is the science of nature, the science of mind, the science of government, the science of morals, so eminently disciplinary, that they all must be carefully explored, that the student must be trained to a careful analysis of their principles, to an accurate discernment of their varied distinctions; and is the infinitely more sublime, the all comprehensive, the momentous science of GOD, so destitute of this quality that it must be ostracised from this brotherhood? Must the Professor, standing at the portals of this magnificent temple, bid the student pass by, telling him that in all its gorgeous halls, there is nothing, absolutely nothing, that will repay even a cursory glance? Surely not. For certainly no study is better suited to promote thorough mental discipline, than the philosophy of philosophies. Can the science of nature, of mind, of government, of morals, present grander themes than the science of GOD, himself the author of nature, the Father of spirits, the source of authority, the foundation and rule of right? What study demands more rapt attention, more profound thought, closer reasoning? What better calculated to expand and ennoble the powers of mind than familiarity with him who fills immensity? What better suited to mortify pride of intellect and teach the most lovely humility, than the study of the being, perfections and works of the infinite One?—at every step the mightiest intellect discerning that he is pressing hard on the unsearchable—is in the immediate presence of him whose ways are past finding out? What better suited to stimulate and at the same time chasten the imagination and refine the taste, than familiarity with the gorgeous imagery of the prophets—than dwelling in the very Holy of Holies of the true, the beautiful, the sublime?

But facts confirm this conclusion. Take a survey of the cultivated intellect of the last eighteen hundred years. Mark the minds that stand pre-eminent above all others for their strength and vigor—the very few giant intellects who have wielded only little less than despotic power. Inquire whence the culture. You find that they derived it mainly from the study of the Bible and its truth. In the school of the Bible were trained Paul, Augustine, Luther, Calvin, Cromwell, Wesley, Whitefield, Edwards, Hall, Chalmers, and hundreds of others, before whom the cultivated mind of the world loves to homage.

But go to the humble walks of life in the lands of the Bible, where it is revered and studied. How often do you find unlettered men and women, ignorant of general literature, ignorant of any science, but such as they have learned from the book of nature, exhibiting a strength of intellect sufficient to grapple with the most abstruse themes; how often do you see them boldly entering realms of thought and discussion, where many a mind boasting its culture, would hesitate to follow? Ask them where they have been trained, what text books they have used, what master has guided them? The Bible has been our school; the Bible our text book; the "spirit of all truth" our teacher, they answer.

I argue no further. The study of the Bible is eminently disciplinary. It does produce the most noble and vigorous intellects, the loftiest culture.

3. Another special end of education is the formation of an elevated moral character.

Man possesses intellectual faculties. Their development and culture is one end of education. Man also possesses moral faculties. The development and culture of these is another end of education of transcendent importance. The proper culture of man's moral faculties produces the elevated moral character I have affirmed to be a special end of education.

This moral character consists in conformity to God's law. Of this law as expounded by the great teacher, the precept, "Thou shalt love the Lord thy God with all thy heart, with all thy soul, and with all thy mind" is the first and great commandment; and the second is like unto it: "Thou shalt love thy neighbor as thyself." This love, permeating a man's entire being, controlling the exercises of the heart, the words of the lips, and the conduct of the life, produces the moral character of which I am speaking. It is the same that adorned our Saviour —simply a Christian character.

The soul pervaded by this principle, shrinks with deep loathing from every base, sinful thing. It seeks with unutterable yearning, after complete and eternal separation from it. It is the determined foe of all wrong, all vice, all crime, all oppression, all misrule. It fights against them even unto death. It cleaves to God and the God-like. It presses on through all difficulties, in the face of all opposition, impelled by an earnest longing after the pure and holy. It is the determined friend of the true and the right. It kindles with unwonted enthusiasm as it looks forward to the day when

"All crimes shall cease and ancient frauds shall fail;
Returning Justice lift aloft her scale:
Peace o'er the world her olive wand extend,
And white-robed Innocence from Heaven descend."

And withal, around it floats the atmosphere of meekness, gentleness and humility.

Such a character, earnest, bold and uncompromising in the right, is the moral character produced by the operation of the law of love in the heart; and such is the moral character to be contemplated in every educational process.

The importance of such a character is obvious. It is at this present time the grand desideratum of every community, of every profession, of all orders and conditions of men. And here at the outset, I would affirm as fundamental the great principle that morality founded on religion, rooted in and growing out of the gospel of the Grace of God, is necessary to the well-being of every community—the foundation of free institutions—essential to their safety and prosperity.

There is a necessity, absolute and uncompromising, that such morality should pervade the body politic. So thought George Washington. In his farewell address he uses the following emphatic words: "Of all the dispositions and habits which

7

lead to political prosperity, religion and morality
are indispensible supports. In vain would that
great man claim the tribute of patriotism, who
should labor to subvert these great pillars of human
happiness, these firmest props of the duties of men
and citizens. The mere politician equally with the
pious man ought to respect and cherish them." So
thought Daniel Webster. In his argument before
the Supreme Court of the United States, in the case
growing out of the late Stephen Girard's will, he
affirms that "the only conservative principle by
which society can be kept together, when crowns
and mitres shall have no more influence, is Religion!
the authority of God! His revealed will and the
influence of the teaching of the ministers of Christianity."

Time will not permit any further illustration of
this position.

If this be true, then the well-being of society, the
permanence and prosperity of our free institutions,
demand that all who occupy positions of responsibility and influence, should possess just this elevated
moral character.

The physician occupies a position of responsibility and influence. He is the guardian of the public health. His influence, too, is extensive and powerful. The position he occupies, and the opportunities he enjoys, give him in many instances the

control of the opinions and conduct of men. His influence ought to be in favor of sound morality, as well as pure and undefiled religion. Surely, then, he ought to maintain a character of spotless purity. His integrity ought to be above suspicion. Men ought to be able to repose in him absolute and unlimited confidence.

The lawyer also occupies a position of responsibility and influence. To him men entrust the care of their property, the vindication of their rights. He often exercises a power little less than absolute over the posessions of others. His influence is well known. No intelligent observer need be told that multitudes bow before it. It is often overpowering. Ought he not, then, to be a man of the purest and loftiest integrity? Ought not his entire conduct to be governed by moral principles that cannot be bought? Is any man, whatever his learning, whatever his talents, whatever his legal ability, fit to be, for an hour, granted a place at the bar, whose maxim is not " Fiat Justitia, si mat cœlum?"

The Statesman, too, occupies a position of great responsibility and commanding influence. The peace and prosperity of the nation are in his hands. Millions of money are at his disposal. Thousands court his favor, cringe and crawl at his feet—happy if he smiles—wretched if he frowns. His words are carried on the wings of the lightning to the remotest corners of the land—multitudes weigh them as the utterance of an oracle, and learn from them what to believe and how to think and act. He has access to springs of influence that control the millions. Surely here. if anywhere, the highest results of the purest morality ought to be found. The Statesman should be planted so firmly in the right, that the combined influence of Gold. Power and Fame could not swerve him a hair's breadth to the right or to the left. There is no place for a corrupt Statesman in a republican government, though, it is to be feared, he is in fact too often found in high places. And his influence, so extensive and so powerful—in what direction should it be exerted? Surely in favor of the true and the right. Shall the Statesman—the man who proposes to conduct the affairs of this mighty nation—exert his influence in any other direction than in behalf of what the " Father of his Country " declared to be indispensible to political prosperity? God forbid.

The teacher, too, occupies a position of responsibility and influence scarce inferior to any other. To him is entrusted the training of the mind, and to a great extent the formation of the character and principles of our people. The masses in every community are very much what the Teacher makes them. What, then, ought to be the character and influence of the teacher? Shall it tend to make men reject religion, disregard its teachings, scorn its solemn sanctions, and trample its obligations under foot? God forbid that any such influence should ever go out from the school. On the contrary, the Teacher, whether his position be in the humblest school or in the proudest university, ought to wear a character of the most elevated morality, and his whole influence, be it as great as it may, should operate to give this same morality the pre-eminence in every heart.

There is still another class of men, whose responsibility and influence are surpassed by few. The author, from the writer of the brief local in the obscurest country weekly, up to the senior editor of the most widely circulated daily; from the writer of a fugitive tale, up to the author of the ponderous tomes that cost years of severe thought and self-denying toil—the man that wields the pen, writes for the million to read, occupies a position of immense responsibility and influence. In many respects, and to a great extent, he forms the principles and directs the conduct of individuals and nations. He, too, should be pure, honest, upright—faithful to the trust committed to him—ever careful to exert his energies in the cause of religion and morality.

Other classes of men might be specified. What has been said, however, is true of all to whom is committed any trust, who wield any influence. The well-being of society, the permanence and prosperity of our free institutions, demand that they all should maintain an elevated morality. Men of wide and powerful influence are usually educated in the college. Here, to a great extent, are formed their principles. Here they are usually made what they are found to be through life. The system of education arranged for the college ought, then to contemplate as an end of pre-eminent importance the formation of an elevated moral character. Any education that secures not this end, however varied and accurate the knowledge it communicates, however complete the intellectual training it affords, is indeed a very doubtful good. There are few present, I venture, who would not rather a thousand fold have their sons and daughters grow up ignorant of the knowledge, and untrained by the discipline of the schools, than that they should enter on life's busy scenes, in the possession of the most magnificent results of the most complete intellectual culture, yet destitute of moral principle—the slaves of wills untaught to bow in homage before the supreme Lord. Men of commanding intellect, in positions of responsibility and influence, without moral principle, are no blessing to any land; a curse, a tremendous curse, rather. It was no canting bigot who said: "The intellectual power, refined to the utmost, and wholly destitute of benevolence, resembles but one being. the principle of evil." Such education makes its subject only a more polished and efficient instrument of Satan. In the language of Everett: "Other objects, important as they are, and filling in their attainment, too often. the highest ambition of parents and children, are in reality but little worth, if unaccompanied by the most precious endowment of our fallen nature, a pure and generous spirit, warmed by kind affection, governed by moral principle, and habitually influenced by motives and hopes that look forward into eternity. It is the first duty and highest merit of a place of education, of whatever name or character—school or college, academical or professional—to unite with all its other working an effort towards the formation of such a character."

But how shall this moral excellence be secured? Instruction in literature and science will not suffice. No man under such regimen has ever attained this elevated moral character. I affirm this as a fact without the slightest fear of successful contradiction. No more will instruction in practical ethics accomplish this end. All experience confirms the principle taught by sound philosophy: "To teach a man his duty is not enough to make him dutiful."

How, then, by what process of culture shall this moral excellence be secured? To answer this question aright we must recur to first principles. It must be remembered as fundamental: 1. That man by nature is depraved, at enmity with God. 2. That his moral character is changed only by the renewing of the Holy Ghost. 3. That this renewal is effected only through the principles of the Gospel as the means.

These facts at this time of day ought to be regarded as axioms by every moral educator. Hence our conclusion is easy. No moral excellence is ever produced, except through the principles of the Gospel as the means, and the Holy Spirit the efficient agent. But the Bible is the only original depository of these principles. If, then. " it is the first duty and highest merit of every place of education, of whatever name or character, to unite with all its other workings an effort towards the formation of such a character," it is the first duty and highest merit of every place of education, especially of every college, to make the principles of the Gospel as set forth in the Bible the subject of regular systematic study. And inasmuch as it is true in the college, as well as in the church, that " neither is he that planteth anything, neither is he that watereth, but God that giveth the increase," the college ought to unite with all its other workings, daily, earnest prayer for the gift of the Spirit, to open the eyes of every understanding, to renew and sanctify every heart.

But it is said by way of objection: " The

necessity of morality is conceded. Yet morality is distinct from religion. A man may be a moral man, and not religious. Your argument for religious instruction therefore fails." I will here stand aside and permit Daniel Webster to reply to this objection in his own burning words: "The ground taken is, that religion is not necessary to morality: that benevolence may be insured by habit, and that all the virtues may flourish and may be safely left to the chance of flourishing, without touching the waters of the living spring of religious responsibility. So the Christian world has not thought; for by that Christian world, throughout its broadest extent, it has been and is held as a fundamental truth that religion is the only solid basis of morals, and that moral instruction not resting on this basis is only building on the sand." "It is all idle, and it is a mockery and an insult to common sense, to maintain that a school for the instruction of youth, from which Christian instruction is sedulously and rigorously shut out, is not deistical and infidel both in its purpose and in its tendency."

I have thus examined the special ends of education. The conclusion we have reached is this : Whether we aim at communicating knowledge, training the intellect, or forming an elevated moral character, we must use the Bible as a text book.

I shall further confirm this principle by reference

to systems of education and the matured judgments of the best educators.

The oldest system of education is the Jewish. It was ordained by God himself. Its character is sufficiently indicated by the following extract from the statute. In regard to the great fundamental principles of religion—Christian as well as Jewish—the Supreme Law-giver thus ordains: "And thou shalt teach them diligently unto thy children. and shalt talk of them when thou sittest in thy house. when thou walkest by the way, and when thou liest down and when thou risest up." (Deut. 6: 7.) From no part of the system of which this is the fundamental law, was religious instruction excluded. The Father of Spirits, who knows the human mind, its condition and necessities, formed this ordinance. It is therefore an authority, that cannot be safely disregarded: an example that ought at all times to be closely followed.

It would be interesting to trace the course of things in this regard from the days of Moses to the present time. We must, however, confine ourselves to the more modern systems.

According to the best systems of education in Europe religious instruction is a part of the course of training in every school.

This is true of England.

After the Reformation, grammar schools were

established all over the kingdom and supported by public. funds. Lord Eldon says that "in these schools care is taken to educate youth in the Christian Religion, and in all of them the New Testament is taught both in Latin and Greek."*

And in 1842, Vice Chancellor Bruce affirms in an important decision the following position: "Courts of equity in this country will not sanction any system of education in which religion is not included."*

To the Scotch system it is only necessary to refer. The very prominent place it has given religious instruction is well known. The experience of centuries has proven the wisdom of the arrangement·

"The instruction of youth in the principles of religion, was made a primary object of the parochial schools."†

The defense and confirmation of the catholic faith that the religion Christian might flourish was a prominent end with which the colleges at St. Andrews were founded.§

At the Reformation the theology of these colleges became protestant; yet religious instruction occupied no lower position after, than before that era. In the act of Parliament establishing the university of Edinburgh, it is declared to be "one colledge of humane letteris and toungis, of philosophie, theolo-

*Quoted in Webster's works, vol. 1, pp. 170, 171.
†McCrie's Life of Knox, p. 87.
§McCrie's Life of A. Melville, p. 359.

gie, medicine, the lawis, and all other liberal sciences. "‡

The Prussian system of education. judged by the principles on which it is founded and the effects it produces, is one of the best in the world. This plan lays down on the foreground of every scheme of studies, as the leading object of every school: "First religious instruction as a means of forming the moral character according to the positive truths of Christianity."

Such too, was the basis of the system of education established by the early fathers of our own country. President Quincy. in his elaborate history of the University at Cambridge—the most ancient college in the United States—tells us, that the "exercises of the students had the aspect of a theological rather than a literary institution. They were practiced twice a day in reading scriptures, giving an account of their experience and proficiency in practical and spiritual truths, accompanied by theoretical observation on the language and logic of the sacred writings. They were carefully to attend public worship, and be examined on their profiting; commonplacing the sermons and repeating them publicly in the hall. " "The studies of the third year included exercises in Hebrew and Syriac. " "In every year and every week of the college course, every class was practised

‡McCrie's life of A. Melville, p. 369, N.
Quoted by McMaster in his Inaug. at M. U. p. 38.

in the Bible and catechetical Divinity. Such were
the principles of education established in the college
under Dunster. Nor does it appear that they were
materially changed during the whole of the seven-
teenth century "* "Every morning a portion of
the Old Testament was read out of Hebrew into
Greek, and every afternoon a portion of the New
Testament out of English into Greek." To obtain
the degree of A. B., a student was required to give
proof of his ability " to read the original of the Old
and New Testament into the Latin tongues, and
resolve them logically."† In 1721 a Professorship
of Divinity was endowed by Thomas Hollis, of
London. Its design was stated in the following
language: "I order and appoint a professor of
Divinity to read lectures in the hall of the college
unto the students." The ordinances assented to and
established by the corporation and Hollis, provide
that the Professor shall give a course of lectures on
systematic and controversial theology, every year—
giving so many lectures weekly as may be necessary to complete the course in that time. In
addition to this he was required to "lecture twice
a week in the hall, on Church History, Jewish
Antiquities, Cases of Conscience, or critical exposition of the Scripture, as he shall judge proper."‡

*Vol. 1, pp. 190, 192.
†Do. p. 571.
‡Vol, 1, pp. 535, 536.

All were required to attend these lectures. From the report of a committee of investigation made in 1723, it appears, "that the Greek Catechism was at that time recited by the freshmen without exposition; Wollebius' and Ames' systems of Divinity, by the other classes, with expositions on Saturday, and repetititions of the sermons of the foregoing Sabbath, by the students on Saturday evenings, when the President was present." In 1776, the plan of study still required "the Divinity Professors to instruct all the scholars in Divinity."‡

"In 1780 the system of the Professor of Divinity included; 1. A dissertation read by the Professor, on some topic of positive or controversial divinity; 2. A catechetical exercise on the preceding lecture accompanied by instructions and remarks." The resident graduates and all the members of the junior or senior classes were required to attend both these exercises. In 1784 it was arranged that none should be required to attend the second exercise but Divinity students. All were required to attend the public lectures.§ Such was the system followed out at Cambridge for nearly two centuries. The same course was pursued. it is believed, without a single exception, in all the colleges in the United States until the opening of the present century. Every college graduate was well trained in theology.

‡Do. p. 133.
II. p. 319.
§Do. 274.

Even as late as 1809 the legislature of Ohio, in the "act to establish Miami University, declared the promotion of religion and morality to be among the objects contemplated in founding that Institution."

Such was the system of education under which the men of position and influence in the early history of our country were trained. We know their character. Their history is safe. We revere their memories. In " times that tried men's souls " they were not found wanting. We sigh as we remember that the race of giants is well nigh extinct.

A new order of things began to be introduced about half a century ago. Religious instruction was felt to be out of place in the college curriculum. Little by little it was eliminated, until it came to be a fact, melancholy yet true, that few of our colleges deserved the name of Christian. And even at this day, in many institutions in our land, the student may comply with every requisition necessary to obtain his degree, and receive no regular instruction in Bible truth. Such a course cannot but be most disastrous in its consequences. Are we not now reaping the bitter fruits of this policy? To what are the troubles that have shaken our political fabric to its very centre, due, more than to the complete destitution of moral principle among many of our public men? and to what is this fact owing but to the godless system of education that has prevailed in time past? The experiment has been tried in India, under circumstances of peculiar interest. Let Dr. Duff tell the story. The following statement was made in 1835: "About eighteen years ago there was founded in Calcutta a college for educating Hindoo youth in the literature and science of Europe, *apart* from religion. The seminary has been attended by persons of rank, wealth and influence in society." The intellectual training was thorough, but no instruction in morals or religion was allowed a place in the institution. And what were the graduates? Dr. Duff tells us, "They were infidels or sceptics of the most perfect kind, believing in nothing, and believing not even in the existence of a Deity, and glorying in their unbelief."† And may we not now see, in the insurrection and wholesale butchery of which we hear such fearful accounts from British India, the legitimate results of this system? The Government in India, in mistaken kindness, has warmed into life in her bosom the viper that is now stinging her to death.

From these records we learn the views of those mighty minds, who formed the systems of education followed for centuries in our own and other lands.

Hear now the deliberate judgments of some of the first minds of our own day, in this regard.

†Duff's speech in the Gen. Ass. of the ch. of S, for 1835.

Says Dr. McMaster, in an address delivered at his inauguration as President of Miami University: " We will not allow ourselves to doubt, that amid a good deal of a jargon of a contrary tenor, the voice of the true people of our land is still, that the system of education in our schools, superior and subordinate, ought to be based on religious instruction."*

The Hon. Edward Everett, in an address delivered on the occasion of his inauguration as President of the University at Cambridge, thus forcibly utters his sentiments: "Moral education is much too important an object to be left to follow as an incidental effect from mere literary culture. It should be deemed the distinct duty of a place of education to form the young to those habits and qualities which win regard and command respect." He then specifies the moral virtues, and adds: "And of those traits of character, I know of no reliable foundation but sincere and fervent religious faith, founded on conviction, enlightened by reason, and nourished by the devout observance of those means of spiritual improvement which Christianity provides. In the faithful performance of this duty, I believe that a place of education in Europe or America renders a higher and more seasonable service to society, at the present day, than by

*p 38.

8

anything that ends in mere scientific and literary culture."*

Daniel Webster, in the argument from which I have already quoted, uses the following language: "In what age, by what sect, where, when, by whom, has religious truth been excluded from the education of youth? Nowhere; never. Everywhere and at all times it has been and is regarded as essential."‡

The late Thomas Grimke, of South Carolina, in his celebrated discourse on "American Education," after characterizing the system prevalent in time past as unchristian, if not anti-christian, and speaking of the importance of religion and morality in a country governed like ours, thus forcibly expounds his views: "It is impossible that Christianity can ever accomplish its object, unless it be made an element of all general education and enter into the daily administration of the whole system. The first great reform is to introduce religion into the every-day instruction of school, academy and college. The Bible should become a text-book from the infant school to the university."†

Prof. Turner, late of Illinois College, in an address before the American Association for the advancement of Science, delivered a year ago at Detroit, reasons thus earnestly: "And when, by *force of*

*Works, vol. 2, 512.
‡Works, 3 p. 152.
†Teachers' Miscellany, p. 373.

education, the great practical truths of the Gospel are made to seize hold of all culture, all learning, all science, all skill, all art, and all work of whatever sort, then, and not till then, shall the glory of the Lord cover the earth as the waters cover the sea; and all forms of Cossack tyranny, and mammon worship, and man worship, and caste worship, and clan worship, and priest worship, and sect worship, and church worship, and the worship of the great Anglo-Saxon God. *respectability*, shall be utterly abolished in these free States, and Jehovah and his Son served and worshiped in spirit and in truth."‡ "We have in our catalogues long lists of authors (mostly heathen, of course), and exercises designed for the culture of the intellectual faculties, followed up by some general stereotyped or clap-trap promise of 'Christianity' and 'paternity' for the discipline of the conscience and will. And where the text-books? Where the daily drill, the apparatus, and the efficient exercises for this greatest of all uses and results? * * * There is an old and venerable book still extant. called the New Testament. Among other things, it contains the sayings and doings of an ANCIENT ONE, who once walked on the plains of Jewry, taught on Mt. Olivet, and who said some very good things about this matter of the conscience and will—so good, that I have sometimes

‡College Review, vol. III, p. 56.

thought it a great pity that the old book should not in some way steal out of the cloisters of the church, and try to take a respectable standing in our college catalogues, alongside of Horace, and Juvenal, and Cicero, and even of good pious Æneas himself. But wise men say it is not classical authority in a Christian land, and I suppose it cannot be done."§

A few words from the Hon. R. C. Winthrop's address before the Association of Alumni of the University at Cambridge, will close these extracts. Speaking of that institution, he says: "And could we but see something of a higher moral discipline, something of a deeper religious sentiment, something of a stronger spiritual influence mingling with the sound scholarship which pervades her halls, and giving something of a fuller and fresher significance to her ancient motto, 'Christo et Ecclesiæ'—could we but see a little more of that state of things here which Thomas Arnold contemplated, when he nobly declared at Rugby: ' It is not necessary that this should be a school of 200, or of 100, or of 50, but it is necessary that it should be a school of Christian gentlemen;' there would be little or nothing more to be desired in her condition." Page 9.

Hence we see the principle I am advocating has not only been recognized by the most approved systems of education; it has also been emphatically

§College Review, III, pp. 55, 56.

affirmed by the great leading minds of the country.

There are, however, objections to my position, which demand at least a passing notice.

One objector reasons thus: "I concede the necessity of the religious instruction of the young. Yet the family, the Sabbath-school and the church are sufficient to secure this end. The methods you recommend are unnecessary." The college is designed for the training of those who propose operating on the *minds* of others. The farmer, the mechanic, the merchant, the man of business, ordinarily obtains an adequate education in the public school and academy. The professional man, of whatever name, requires a higher education. To supply this the college is organized. Now if, for this class of men a more complete and thorough training is required in other departments, is not the same, at least, as necessary in the department of religious instruction? Does he not need more extensive knowledge in this department, as well as in any other —a more elevated morality as well as more thorough discipline—and for all these ends is not more thorough discipline—and for all these ends is not more thorough drill in the study of the Bible as necessary as in the study of languages, mathematics and philosophy?

Besides, if religious instruction be at all of the importance it appears to be, it will not do to dispose of it thus summarily.

Shall the Professor spend six days in the week drilling the student in the principles of general literature and science, deeming all this necessary to secure the knowledge and discipline the student needs, and never once open the Bible to teach therefrom an infinitely higher knowledge than that to be found in any book of science or literature—a knowledge absolutely necessary to develop that moral excellence we have seen to be of such pre-eminent worth, deeming the instruction of the family, the Sabbath-school and the church, on a portion of one day in the seven, enough for all this? No, no—a thousand times, no.

Another objects: "Colleges will then be sectarian." If by this it is meant that every college will advance the interests of some one denomination of Christians more than another, I grant it. Still more. I claim that in this sense ALL colleges, be they nominally what they may, are, and of necessity must be, sectarian. If, however, it is meant that the imparting of religious instruction is impossible without making the college an instrument for proselyting the student, I deny it. It is certainly a possible thing for a college faculty to teach Bible truth, fully and clearly, and at the same time give reasonable offense to none. I think I may safely appeal to the students of Monmouth College, to testify, if here in the Bible recitation the whole counsel of God has not been faithfully declared; and I feel sure not a student will complain that in any particular there has been any interference with his denominational preferences. And here let me again quote from the earnest words of Professor Turner: " Christianity is no more sectarianism than the law of gravitation is, and it is equally demonstrable that the world is inevitably Cossack without the one as it is chaos without the other. The world has long enough left this Christianity to swing and dangle in mid-air, among mere probable truths, or buried it a thousand fathoms deep under the accumulated mud and slime of skeptic, priest and sect."

Suppose, however, it is true that colleges can not impart the needed religious instruction without becoming sectarian: what then? Unhesitatingly and emphatically I answer, let them be sectarian; sectarian a thousand times over, rather than unchristian. I do believe the importance of a complete and thorough course of religious instruction to be so great, that it ought to be secured at all hazard, even though every college in the land should be baptized with the most intense sectarianism.—And here I again invite you to listen to the eloquent words of Mr. Winthrop. Speaking of the university at Cambridge, he says: "Better, a thousand fold better, that a seminary like this should be under the steady, effective—aye, or even exclusive—influ-

ence of any one religious sect, than that it should
be without the influence of some sort of vital Christianity.   *   *   *   But let us be cautious,
that in attempting to shut out any one particular
ray which may be imagined to predominate in our
academic atmosphere, we take no risk of shutting
out the glorious sunshine of the Gospel, and leaving
the institution in this day of its highest intellectual
advantages in a condition of spiritual darkness;

Dark, dark, dark, amid the blaze of noon."

Again it is objected: "There is not time for so
much religious instruction during the college course."
Not time!   So much time is needed for the study of
Virgil, Horace, and Cicero; of Xenophon, Homer
and Plato, that there is no time for the Bible!   So
much time is needed for the study of lines and
angles—of quantities, negative and positive, known
and unknown, variable and constant, that there is no
time for the study of man's relations to his fellow
man, to his God, to eternity!   So much time is
needed for the philosophy of things created, that
there is no time for the philosophy of the Creator!
Away with such absurdity!   Let the mighty themes
of God's own book have their due place in the college curriculum, crowd out thence what it may.   Can
it for a moment be supposed that the student would
sustain any loss who would read a little less of Livy

and Herodotus, and a little more of Gospels; a little less of Horace and Homer, and a little more of David and Isaiah; a little less of Cicero and Plato, and a little more of Paul and John; study a little less the relations of time, and a little more the relations of eternity; a little less the philosophy of man, and a little more the philosophy of God; spend a little less time in the cultivation of the intellect, and a little more on the cultivation of the heart? Would not such a change, on the contrary, be eminently favorable to the student's best interests? If there is no room for the Bible in the college curriculum, make room. Such is the verdict of common sense.

At the meeting of the Synod of Illinois, of the A. R. P. Church, at which Monmouth College was taken under its care, the Board of Trust then appointed was instructed: "While it is careful to prevent interference with the denominational preferences of the students, to take order that such instruction in the Word of God may be given as may be necessary to secure the ends of a thorough education." At the next meeting of the Board, a course of study and code of laws was adopted. In these the principles I have advocated to-day were fully recognized and formally approved. The Bible has been made a text book in the college. According to the ordinances then adopted, the students, in addition to the usual Sabbath exercises, in whatever church they themselves or those acting for them may choose, all, from the first to the last of their connection with the college, must attend a regular Bible recitation. Every student that completes the full course will be drilled in the great principles of religion and morals, as regularly and as faithfully as in any subject of literature and science. These ordinances have already been put into execution. And now, formally entering on the office to which you, gentlemen of the Board, have called me, I do engage, before God and this witnessing assembly, to continue to faithfully execute the same. No effort shall be spared to communicate to the students as extensive and valuable learning as is compatible with more important ends; to secure to the students, by the use of the long-tried methods, the most complete and thorough intellectual culture; and while due care is taken not to interfere with the denominational preferences of any, at least equal care shall be taken to give such instruction in the Word of God as may be necessary to secure the highest moral excellence. And believing that a prosperous institution, faithfully conducted on these principles, cannot fail to be a fountain whence shall gush forth streams of living waters, for which "the wilderness and solitary place shall be glad and the desert shall rejoice and blossom as the rose," I to-day call upon you all to lend a helping hand to plant our college on a firm foundation, and furnish it with all the instrumentalities necessary to qualify it for the most extensive usefulness. The intellectual and moral wants of our sons and daughters— of the teeming millions that shall one day throng these broad prairies—forbid us to hesitate. A solemn trust has been committed to us; God grant that we may be found faithful. Believing, too, that the excellency of the power is of God, that we need his spiritual presence in the chapel and the class-room. no less than in the church, that we may to any good degree gain the high ends we contemplate, I call upon you, Christian men and women, to pray for our college. From out thousands of earnest, devoted hearts, let daily petitions rise to our Father in Heaven. that we all, Board of Trust, Faculty and Students, may be blessed and made a blessing— that those who go forth from among us may be richly furnished with the most important wisdom and knowledge—that their powers may be developed by the highest culture—that, above all, they may be adorned with the beauties of holiness, eminently good and mighty to do good; that Monmouth College, be its students few or many, may be truly a Christian College.

WALKING IN THE TRUTH.

The Baccalaureate Sermon, delivered before the graduating class of 1877.

" For I rejoice greatly, when the brethren came and testified of the truth that is in thee, even as thou walkest in the truth. I have no greater joy than to hear that my children walk in truth."– III John, 3, 4.

When years ago you entered college and commenced your course, you hardly dared look forward to its completion. The years, however, have come and gone; years of work and warfare, defeat and triumph, joy and sorrow. You have at last finished the studies required here, and passed your examination; and, now, it only remains that we should address you a few parting words, place in your hands the parchment which you have fairly won, and give you our blessing.

The words which I have chosen as the theme of discourse to-day, have been taken from a brief note addressed by the Apostle John to the well beloved Gaius. In it he speaks of his joy when he heard that Gaius had received the truth and was walking in it; and declared that he had no greater joy than that which came from knowing that his children were walking in the truth. John but expresses the common sentiment of the followers of Christ. Wherever you find a Christian man or woman, you

(124)

find one who rejoices greatly when tidings come, that their well beloved, have received the truth into their hearts and are practicing it in their lives.

In addressing you to-day, I desire to remind you that Monmouth College has no greater joy than to hear that her children are walking in the truth, and to press on you its claims. I have nothing new to say. My discourse will be but little more than a resume of the instructions of the class room, and of the chapel to which you have been listening all these years.

I. But what truth is that of which John speaks? I answer, it is called, "the truth," "the doctrine of Christ." "the truth as it is in Jesus," the system known as "Christianity." Again, it may be asked, What is Christianity? This question is pertinent; I shall attempt to answer it briefly.

1. Christianity is a Doctrine. It is a doctrine concerning God. It teaches that the Father, Son and Holy Ghost—three persons—constitute one God, "infinite, eternal, and unchangeable in his being, wisdom, power, holiness, justice, goodness and truth;" and emphasizing two great facts: First, "that justice and judgment are the habitation of his throne," and, second, "that the Lord God is merciful and gracious, long suffering and abundant in goodness and truth, keeping mercy for thousands, forgiving iniquity and transgression and sin." It

is a doctrine concerning man; teaching that he is a creature of God, and subject to his authority, as supreme and absolute, and emphasizing the great facts, that God made man upright, but that he had fallen, and was by nature a sinner, lost and ruined, condemned and helpless. It is pre-eminently a doctrine concerning salvation; teaching that the Father manifests his love for man by giving his Son to be the propitiation for sin; that the Son loved us and gave himself for an offering and a sacrifice to God, and thus purchased full and complete redemption for us, so that God may still be just and the sinner saved; and that all this magnificent inheritance, is imparted to the people of God by the office and work of his Holy Spirit; thus laying the foundation for the glorious Gospel of the grace of God, which proclaims the gift to the world of a present, and all-sufficient Saviour, and authorizes every sinner who hears, to receive him as his own, and in him a salvation fully commensurate with the wants of the most needy. Such is the doctrine of Christianity.

2. Christianity is a Law. Its fundamental statute has been stated thus by its great law-giver: "Thou shalt love the Lord thy God, with all thy heart, and with all thy soul, and with all thy mind. This is the first and great commandment: and the second is like unto it: thou shalt love thy neighbor

as thyself." It is a law requiring faith and love, reverence and devotion, submission and obedience God-ward. It is a law requiring purity in all our thoughts, words, and actions; holiness in all manner of conversation. · It is a law requiring diligent and earnest use of all the ordinances chosen and appointed of God as means to holiness, righteousness and purity. It is a law demanding watchfulness against the devil, the world and the flesh, and every influence that tends to draw men down from holy living, and away from the paths of righteousness. Such is the law of Christianity.

Christianity is a Life. It is a life begun in the new creation: a life of faith in God manifest in the flesh; a life of love to God manifest in the flesh, the perfection of all beauty and goodness; a life regulated by a law which is holy; a commandment which is holy, just and good; a life of self-denial, " teaching us that, denying ungodliness and worldly lusts, we should live soberly, righteously and godly in this present world;" a life whose end is the glory of God in the welfare of men; a life of peace, joy and happiness as far as attainable in a world of sin and sorrow; a life of service in the cause of the King of kings and Lord of lords: a life of glory, honor and immortality, begun in time and perpetuated throughout eternity. Such is the Christian Life, defined by the Master, and more or less perfectly exhibited by his followers.

4. Christianity is an Inspiration. It finds man of the earth, earthy, dead in sin. It breathes into him the breath of life and he becomes a living soul. The Holy Spirit takes up his abode in him and he becomes a temple of the living God. It puts within him the same mind which was also in Christ Jesus. It fills him with the purest sentiment and loftiest aspirations. It inspires him with a holy ambition after personal excellence; "whatsoever things are true, whatsoever things are honest, whatsoever things are just, whatsoever things are lovely, whatsoever things are of good report; if there be any virtue, if there be any praise," he thinks of these things. All knowledge, all skill, all power, all " best gifts," such as qualify man for royal work in the service of God and man, he covets earnestly. It often inspires him with yearnings, unutterable, and nerves him to efforts, herculean—perfect godlikeness. Such is the spirit which Christianity breathes into men. In so far as man takes it into his heart, in so far he is animated, nerved, and controlled by this spirit.

5. Christianity is a Hope. It finds man in despair; in so far as he receives, trusts, loves and serves the Christ of Christianity, it fills him with hope. It fills him with hope for himself; hope of an abiding peace with God; of a useful and honorable life; of a happy death; and of a glorious immortality. It fills him with hope for his fellow

men; hope for the overthrow of the kingdom of darkness, of iniquity, transgression and sin, and for the establishment of the kingdom of light, of peace, of purity and of righteousness; hope for the speedy coming of the day, when

" All crimes shall cease
And ancient frauds shall fail;
Returning justice lift aloft her scale,
And white-robed innocence descend."

Hope for a new heaven and a new earth, wherein dwelleth righteousness; the coming of the time when the air of heaven, as men breathe it, shall not pass through bodies that have been polluted by sin; when the food which the earth furnishes shall not be used to pamper the bodies of those who give no thanks to God, and to nourish and strengthen that which shall be expended in breaking his laws, and in dishonoring his name; when the sun shall light mankind on errands of love, and no more shed its beams on the evil and unjust as they prosecute their schemes of aggrandizement; and the moon and the stars shall not look down on deeds of criminality which dare not face the light of day. Such are the glorious hopes with which the Christ of Christianity fills its disciples.

It is a life moulded by these doctrines, regulated by this law, inspired by these sentiments and aspirations, and animated by these hopes, that Monmouth

9

College desires her children to live: when they walk in this truth, she rejoices.

II. But is this system—this Christianity—true? Is it only a myth, a creation of the imagination, a fond delusion, the product of human longings, the baseless fabric of a dream, and no more. Or, is it a a simple fact—one of the eternal verities of things in which man may safely trust? This is the question before which all others drop into insignificance. Over it have been fought the battles of the ages. Around it rage the fiercest struggles of the present. Let us look and see what the truth is. Lies cause men to err. Monmouth College rejoices when her children walk in the truth. The question is simply this: Does this system, which we call Christianity, stand the test of truth? Let us apply them and see:

1. The first of these tests is Intuition. Does Christianity commend itself to pure reason? Some principles we see to be false; we do not need any proof to satisfy us that they are untrue. As soon as they are understood, all men everywhere pronounce them false. For example, the half is greater than the whole. " A proposition can be both true and false." "Injustice is right." No man needs proof to convince him that such principles are false. Now, any system based upon principles, which all men intuitively discern to be false, is itself false and must be

rejected. All systems of truth are built on axioms, true in the last analysis. Every one of them commends itself to our reason as not false, but true. Now, test the fundamental principles, the axioms of Christianity, bring them out in the broad daylight; let there be no perversions, no exaggerations, no distortions; let them be stated clearly and correctly and then test them. Time would fail me to enumerate these axioms, but make the trial for yourselves. Be as critical, as acute, as impartial as the love of truth can make you. Go through the doctrines, the law, the life, the inspiration, the hope of Christianity, with your measuring reed. Do perfect work. Christianity fears nothing from careful investigation and thorough scrutiny. It is only the partial observer, the hasty generalizer that excites her apprehension. He who makes such an investigation can make but one report: "The law is holy and the commandments holy and just and good." Not one of the fundamental principles of Christianity will be rejected; every one of them will be approved.

2. The second of these tests is Consistency. Is Christianity consistent? Consistent with its claims as a divine system with; itself; with all known truth? (1). Christianity challenges belief as a divine system. Its great teacher claimed to be divine, and to have come forth from the Father.

He taught as one having authority. His Apostles claimed to speak in the name of God. Christianity is either divine, or a base imposture from God, or it is a lie. Now, is it worthy of God? Many object to salvation by grace. They affirm that it is unfriendly to godliness and righteousness. They reason on this wise: A holy God cannot save men in a way that will encourage sin. The salvation of a wicked, rebellious and undeserving sinner wholly by grace, tends to encourage sin and is, therefore, unworthy of God. But is it so? Salvation deserved, salvation as the reward of merit, is impossible. Can any man tell what penalty a single sin against a God, to whom we are all under infinite obligation, merits? Can any man figure up the punishment merited by a life of rebellion and sin? Can a sinner then merit anything? Who is he with intellect so blinded and conscience so hardened as to appear before God, claiming a salvation he has merited? Where is the mortal so presumptuous! Even the cherubim veil their faces with their wings in presence of a God of spotless holiness; and shall man, with his little, venture into his presence chamber, claiming glory, honor and immortality as the pay for a holy life? Away with such a preposterous thought. Sound philosophy scorns such absurdities. Salvation cannot be by the deeds of the law.

Grace, however, becomes a king. Never does royalty appear more truly royal, than when dispensing favor. When you appeal to the deepest and truest convictions of the human heart, you receive the response: Grace, free grace, abounding grace, is worthy of the God of heaven and of earth. God gives with an open hand in nature; all his laws are freighted with unmerited blessings for man. His administration is gracious. When, then, Christianity comes and testifies, " By grace are ye saved, through faith, and that not of yourselves; it is the gift of God," does it prove Christianity unworthy of God?

But more: A system of grace most powerfully appeals to the human heart, and most surely awakens and stimulates right affections toward God. How often has the culprit, hardened by punishment, been reformed by grace? Salvation by grace secures holiness as no other scheme can. God pardons that he may deliver and sanctify.

Again, many object to salvation by blood. They do not like the scarlet thread running through Christianity. They find symbols of blood in the law; songs of blood in the psalms; predictions of blood in the prophets; the story of blood in the gospels; the philosophy of blood in the epistles; and the triumph of blood in the apocalypse. It offends them. They sneer at it as a bloody religion. They turn from it in disgust. But why? The blood of Christ is the symbol of his obedience unto death. His death was not for himself. Upon him with the consent of the Father, and with his own consent, were laid the iniquities of us all. "He bare our sins in his own body on the tree." He took our place, and suffered "the just for the unjust, that he might bring us to God." Now what is there in this unworthy of God? He will save none at the expense of justice. The Judge of all the earth must do right. But in the Son we find a willing substitute for his people, bearing their sins and redeeming them. Men are familiar with the idea of substitution. It is everywhere seen in the arrangements of society. One man does for his friend, what that friend cannot do for himself. The security pays the debt of the principal. Everywhere blessings come to the unworthy through the mediation of the worthy. God has imbedded this principle in the constitution of man and of society. We find it fundamental in Christianity. Is it therefore not of God? Is it unworthy of him to provide and accept a substitute for man?

But men complain of it as unintelligible. True; there are many things in it too high for human intellect, while these principles and precepts which man must understand that he may be saved, are so simple and plain that a child can grasp them. Even these are running out into incomprehensible mysteries. Is Christianity unworthy of God because it soars to immeasurable heights? We are finite; can we grasp the infinite? Look around; you are moving in mystery. The human you cannot grasp; the divine you cannot. You can know of it; but to comprehend it is impossible. Mystery is a mark of the divine. Christianity comes to us with its fathomless depths and cloud-capped heights; shall we pronounce it unworthy of God because we cannot understand its immensities? Nay: can I comprehend Christianity as I can a human philosophy? I would reject it as an imposture. The infinite must be incomprehensible by the finite; the divine by the human.

(2.) But if Christianity is true it is self-consistent. Is it?

This is a hard test. Many writers, in many lands. in distant ages have set forth this system. In calm history; in the flights of sublime poetry; in the bold symbols of prophecy; in the similitude of parables and allegory; in the profound discussion of philosophy, its principles have been exhibited; one here, another there; one phase of this, another of that. When of all these diverse utterances we demand that they shall be self-consistent, as the expression of the thoughts of a single mind, we apply a test which no false system can stand. The question is, Does Christianity stand this test? I answer: It must stand it or be condemned. To be proved self-contradictory is to be proved false. To make out this charge against Christianity, it is not sufficient to show that some things in it are incomprehensible and their consistency unintelligible. No man may be able to comprehend how three consist in one God-head, and yet, they may thus co-exist. This statement accords with all analogy. Co-existence is to be found everywhere, the mode of which no man professes to explain. To prove Christianity self-contradictory, it must be shown that it affirms facts and principles both of which *cannot possibly be true.*

Now man has been trying to prove Christianity contradictory for more than two thousand years. Have they succeeded? By misrepresentation and distortion, by exaggeration and equivocation, they have made it appear *as if* they had found the much sought contradictions. But millions of the clearest, of the most acute, and most logical minds that have adorned our race, have declared and most firmly believed, that no such contradictions have been proved; more, that no such contradictions exist. Christianity is self-consistent.

(3.) But is Christianity consistent with other truth? This is a still harder test. If our religion is false, it certainly cannot pass this ordeal. But what are the facts? Men have exhausted their energies to find facts inconsistent with the facts of

Christianity, and with what result? They have diligently searched the heavens; bored deep down into the strata of the earth and questioned these fossils; they have dredged the bottom of the ocean; they have placed the microscope animalculæ on the witness stand; they have talked with atoms and protoplasm; they have raked up the debris of kitchen heaps, and of like dwellings; they have figured on the ages of stone, and of bronze, of bone and of iron; they have measured the mud of the Nile, and carefully analyzed its contents; they have deciphered the inscriptions on old monuments; examined the most ancient records of all religions from the Vedas to the Book of Mormon; they have sought to unlock the hidden mysteries of all languages and speech, in the hope of finding somewhere, a fact of some sort, that would give the lie to the teachings of Christianity, and with what result? Many deductions that men have drawn from Bible facts, have been proven false; many theories woven together to explain Bible mysteries have been exploded; many human speculations have been proved worthless, but, after all this very costly and laborious work, still not one fact has been established, that gives the lie to the Christian system. It stands to-day a consistent portion of eternal truth.

3. The third test is Adaptation. Is Christianity suitable to man? Is it adapted to the ends which

it is intended to accomplish? Every system of
truth must stand this test. Does Christianity? I
answer: It professes to supply man's spiritual needs
and to be adapted to this end. Now what are these
needs, and what are the adaptations of Christianity
to them?

(1.) Man needs the knowledge of certain truths,
and deep convictions in respect to them. Christianity embodies these and challenges human belief
on the authority of God. The man who believes in
Christ as a Saviour, and accepts his teachings is at
rest in respect to that immense mass of truth, as he
can never be from the mere inductions of reason.

(2.) Man needs reconciliation to God. In Christianity the way of peace is opened up through the
blood of the cross. From the very nature of the
case, he who trusts in that blood, as he is warranted
to do, must be at peace.

(3.) Man needs forgiveness. Christianity opens
the way by which God can be just and the justifier
of him which believeth in Jesus. He who believes
the record and accepts and trusts the Saviour as
offered in the gospel, must know the blessedness of
him whose transgression is forgiven and whose sin
is covered.

(4.) Man needs holiness. Christianity was meant
to save men from their sins. To this end Christ himself came, suffered and died, and now administers

the government entrusted to him. "Christ also loved the church, and gave himself for it; that He might sanctify and cleanse it with the washing of water by the word, that he might present to himself a glorious church, not having spot, or wrinkle, or any such thing: but that it might be holy and without blemish." Christianity gives men a perfect law; there is no defect, to be found in it. It presses upon him the strongest motives. Pleading with him to depart from all iniquity, it appeals to the strongest fears, the brightest hopes, the loftiest aspirations, the most potent sentiments that can exist in the human heart, or operate on the human life. It is impossible to place man under stronger motives to holiness than those which Christianity furnishes. And in addition to all this, it reveals an omnipotent helper; one able to save to the very uttermost. He who imbibes the spirit of Christianity, adopts its principles, and walks by its law, is holy.

(5.) Man needs support, comfort and encouragement.

All this Christianity furnishes. In Christ " all fulness dwells." In him we may find the supply of all our needs. Trusting in Christ according to the word of promise, we receive grace for grace.

Christianity is suited to man. As a system of means, it is adapted to the ends it was intended to accomplish.

4. My fourth test is Comparison. Is there anything better—any system of religion that teaches better doctrines, a holier law, a purer or more exalted life, that breathes a more God-like spirit, or opens up to its believers more glorious prospects? If so, what is it? Is there any system of religion known to man for which we would, for a moment, think of bartering away the religion of Christ? Shall we give up and accept in its stead Mormonism? Or, shall we adopt Mohammedanism as our religion? Or, shall we go to Confucius and learn of him, the faith, the law, the life, the inspiration and the hope that has made China what it is? Or, shall we enter the school of Brahma, and become disciples of the idolatry. the polytheism, and the pantheism of the Hindoos? Or, shall we say Gotama is our master and Buddhism our faith? Or, shall we resurrect some one of the religions buried in the ruins of the past? Which one of all the religions that exist, or ever have existed, shall we accept as superior to Christianity? Take their several books and study them well; go into their temples and study well the worship conducted there; go out among the people, and examine carefully the principles which govern them, the lives they are living. the spirit that animates them, and the hopes that cheer them: make up your verdict carefully, thoughtfully, patiently; render it. candidly,

what shall it be? Ah, there can be no question. Christianity, a thousand times over, rather than any of them.

But there is a religion called "Deism." It contains two articles of faith: First, there is a God; second, Christianity is untrue. Its simplicity commends it. One of its greatest lights, Thomas Paine, affirms "that it teaches without the possibility of being mistaken, all that is necessary or proper to be known." Certainly a religion of which this is true is what we need, and all we need. But is this true of Deism? It has no great Prophet to outline its principles, and its disciples are agreed in absolutely nothing, except in the dogmas already stated.

Read over the pages of history and see what sort of results have been produced by this faith. Shall we give up Christianity and accept Deism? What then? It comes to this: Christianity or nothing. The rejection of Christianity ends practically in Atheism. We may begin with "Not this man, but Barabbas," but we will end with the dogma, "There is no God." The alternative is Christianity or Atheism, and it is between these two systems that the conflict rages to-day.

(5.) I come now to my last test—Experiment. Christianity challenges its application The Great Teacher declared, "If any man will do his will, he shall know of the doctrine whether it be of God."

Everywhere the unbeliever is called upon to test and see. More still; it is capable of trial at every point. If it were mere speculation, pure dogma and nothing more, it would be utterly incapable of being put on trial. But it is eminently practical. making the broadest declarations and holding out magnificent promises, so that its disciples are constantly testing it. It is always and everywhere on trial; and with what results. Let us see.

(1). Apply the national test. "Righteousness exalteth a nation: sin is a reproach to any people." Now what are the facts? The purer, the more truly Biblical the Christianity of any people, the more generally it is accepted; the more thoroughly they are imbued with it; the more completely they live it out: the happier and more prosperous they are; the higher and more nearly perfect their civilization.

(2). Apply individual tests. (a). "Come unto me, all ye that labor and are heavy laden, and I will give you rest." Now what is the fact? Simply this: Multitudes have come to Christ and found rest; multitudes are coming to Christ and finding rest; every soul of man, no matter where he lives, or who, or what he is, that does come to Christ, does find rest, in so far as they trust him. (b). It aims and promises to make those who receive and trust in Christ, holy. He is called Jesus, because he saves his people from their sins. Now what are the facts?

Faith in Christ does work by love; it does purify the heart; it does overcome the world. Multitudes testify that through faith in Christ they have been saved from sins. During the last few months, a great cloud of witnesses have arisen, and in the most public manner, the most decided and outspoken manner, have testified that by the power of the Christ of Christianity they have been saved from besetting sins that had brought them to the brink of perdition. And, let men say what they please of the inconsistencies of Christians and churches, every godly man and woman in the land, every Christian church, walking in the truth, in the midst of a wicked and perverse generation, a generation abounding in corruption, is a standing testimony to the purifying power of Christianity. It makes good all its promises. (c). But there is also the promise of answers to prayer. Search and find out the kind of prayer to which an answer is promised. Mark well each characteristic. Search and find out the promises. See just what they are, and mark them well. Now look through the record and you will find that God answered such prayers, before the coming of Christ; that God answered such prayers in apostolic times; that God has answered such prayers ever since, and that he is answering such prayers now. More, a single case cannot be made out in which a true prayer has ever failed to be answered. Men have had faith in prayer in all ages; they have faith still; never was this faith more general or stronger than it is to-day. What means the crowded meetings for prayer all over the land? Thronged not with the ignorant, the superstitious, the fanatical, but with the intelligent, the thoughtful and the practical—men and women who waste no time on that which does not pay. The increasing millions of praying Christians are gathering hosts of witnesses to the power of prayer. Prayer is answered.

Let these examples suffice. Christianity stands the test of experiment. What then is the conclusion of the whole matter? Pure reason finds no fundamental principle false; every axiom involved in it, it pronounces true. It is consistent with its claims as a Divine religion; with itself; with all known truth. It is suited to man and to the ends which it was intended to accomplish. It is superior to all competing systems. There is nothing better. It is this or nothing. It stands the test of experiment. On trial, it proves itself all that it claims to be. Is it any wonder that John wrote to the well beloved Gaius in the terms of my text? Is it any wonder that Monmouth College should have no greater joy than to hear that her children are walking in the truth?

And now my dear Seniors, suffer a word of exhortation: Study this heaven-born system of

religion; master it thoroughly; aim at a full understanding of its doctrines, its laws, its life, its spirit
and its hopes. Believe in it more firmly; seek for
deeper and deeper convictions of its truth; obey its
law more faithfully; live its life more perfectly; be
filled with its spirit and its hopes. Hold it fast,
never give it up: give up all else first; die first.
Many will stand up against you, still stand fast in
the Lord. Speak out for it. Let neither man nor
devil frighten you into cowardly silence, when faithfulness to truth and righteousness require you to
speak out. Don't be cowards. Work hard for it.
You expect hard work; but work for what you may,
let it be in Christ's service and in Christ's cause.

I am done; craving your pardon for my mistakes
and shortcomings as your friend, guardian and
instructor; thanking you for all the joy I have had
with you, and help I have received from you in
advancing the Master's cause here; remembering
that your Senior year has been a year of the right
hand of the Son of Man, in our beloved college, and
that the class of '77 has indeed been a blessing to
it, and praying for you, grace, mercy and peace, I
bid you go, gathering assuredly that a covenant
keeping God will be with you still, and bless you
abundantly.

WHAT MUST I DO TO BE SAVED?

The answer to this question is of vital importance to two classes; to sinners enquiring after salvation and to the teacher instructing the ignorant. Desiring to help both, I write this article.

I. We all need salvation because we are sinners, and being sinners, we are by nature, under wrath. We need salvation from wrath, from sin, from trouble, from ignorance, from weakness, from many evils.

II. The salvation we need has been purchased by Christ, is in him and must be obtained from him: "neither by the blood of goats and calves, but by his own blood, he entered in once into the holy place, having obtained eternal redemption for us." "Who gave himself for us that he might redeem us from all iniquity, and purify unto himself a peculiar people zealous of good works." "Forasmuch as ye know that ye were * * * redeemed * * * with the precious blood of Christ." "For it pleased the Father that in him should all fulness dwell." "In whom are hid all the treasures of wisdom and knowledge." "In whom we have redemption .through his blood, even the forgiveness of sins."

"And this is the record, that God hath given us

eternal life, and this life is in his Son." "He hath
made us accepted in the beloved." "Who hath
blessed us with all spiritual blessings in heavenly
places in Christ Jesus." "But my God shall supply
all your need according to his riches in glory by
Christ Jesus." Our Saviour, the Lord Jesus Christ,
has purchased and holds in trust for them who
believe, all the treasures of wisdom and knowledge,
forgiveness, acceptance, life, and the supply of all
our need, all spiritual blessings. The question next
arises, How are we to obtain and enjoy this great
salvation? I answer:

III. Not by works of righteousness which we
may do, or can do. Salvation is expressly denied to
all on such grounds. By the deeds of the law there
shall be no flesh justified in his sight. "A man is
not justified by the works of the law." "Not by
works of righteousness which we have done, but
according to his mercy he saved us." Nowhere is
obedience to the law made the condition on which
the impartation to man of the blessings in Christ
depends. It is not, therefore, correct to bid the
sinner—

1. Reform his life as the condition of salvation.
It is not offered on this condition. Men may reform
in the common acceptation of the term, and perish.
Outward conformity to the precepts of the second
table of the law, may consist with ungodliness in
the heart.

2. It is not correct to bid the sinner live a religious life, read his Bible, say prayers, go to religious meetings, unite with the church, go to the sacrament, or do any thing of the kind as the condition of acceptance with God. Salvation is not promised on any such conditions. Men may do all these things and perish. "Not every one that saith unto me, Lord, Lord, shall enter into the kingdom of heaven." "Many will say unto me in that day, Lord, Lord, have we not prophesied in thy name? and in thy name have cast out devils? and in thy name done many wonderful works? And then will I confess unto them, I never knew you; depart from me, ye that work iniquity."

3. It is not correct to bid the sinner give large money to supply the wants of the needy, or perform great works, or make great sacrifices in the services of Christ the condition of acceptance. Salvation is not offered on such terms. Men may comply with them and perish. "Though I bestow all my goods to feed the poor, and though I give my body to be burned and have not charity it profiteth me nothing."

4. It is not correct to bid the sinner get knowledge and understanding as a condition of acceptance with God. Salvation is nowhere offered on such terms. A man may be very familiar with the Bible, understand well its doctrines and its precepts, be

orthodox in his belief, a giant in defense of the truth, and very zealous in propagating it, and still perish. "Though I have the gift of prophecy and understand all mysteries and all knowledge * * * * and have not charity I am nothing." To this line of reasoning it may be objected that in Micah vi: 8, a different doctrine is taught. "He hath showed thee, O man, what is good; and what doth the Lord require of thee, but to do justly, and to love mercy and to walk humbly with thy God." I answer: It is evident from the context that these words are the answer of Balaam to the inquiries of Balak recorded in the sixth and seventh verses, and are to be regarded as the gospel according to Balaam, the best answer that he could give to the questions of the king; and not a statement of the very gospel of the grace of God. But if we do regard these words as the words of Micah, still we cannot obtain an interest in the blessings in Christ in this way. For who of all the children of men can come before the Lord, and plead that they have complied with these conditions, and are, therefore, entitled to the blessings of salvation? If there is, therefore, no other way, none can be saved. The Lord be praised, however, "there is a more excellent way."

Again it may be said, that our Lord declares that " he that doeth the will of my Father which is in heaven," shall enter into the kingdom of God. But the question is, What is the will of our Father in heaven, in relation to the matter of obtaining salvation? He expressly declares that it is not by works of righteousness. It remains to be seen what it is. However, let me not be misunderstood. The Lord requires of us holy living, religious service, work in his vineyard, knowledge and understanding, but not as conditions of salvation. Godly living and a holy service are the results and evidences of acceptance, and not the grounds or reasons of it.

IV. The true answer was given by Paul and Silas to the jailer, "Believe upon the Lord Jesus Christ and thou shalt be saved." The following scriptures clearly teach it: "And this is the record, that God hath given us eternal life and this life is in his Son." "But to as many as received him, to them gave he the power to become the sons of God. even to them that believe upon his name." "Ho, every one that thirsteth. come ye to the waters, and he that hath no money; come ye, buy and eat, yea, come, buy wine and milk, without money and without price." "Whosoever will, let him take the water of life freely." "For God so loved the world that he gave his only begotten son that whosoever believeth on him should not perish but have everlasting life." Now what do these scriptures mean?

1. God hath given or granted to sinners, Christ to be their Saviour and in him a full. free, present

salvation. This is the record God hath given us concerning his son. It is the grand fact of the gospel.

2. This record we are required to believe—believe that it is indeed true, that this grant has been made to us: and that there is for us in Christ all the salvation we need.

3. The most important act on our part, corresponding to this grant, is receiving Christ as he is offered to us in the gospel. Receiving Christ he and all the'salvation that is in him becomes ours. At once he is made unto us " wisdom and righteousness, and sanctification and redemption;" " we are complete in him." We have in him, not in our own fruition, but in him, forgiveness. holiness, consolation, wisdom, strength, the supply of all our need. Let it be carefully noticed that the moment we receive Christ he becomes ours, and with him the redemption that is in him.

4. These scriptures also teach that we are required to trust in him for the salvation which he has purchased for his people. It is our duty to trust him for forgiveness. sanctification. consolation, wisdom. strength, grace to help in time of need.

The child to whom his father has willed $100,000, possesses the inheritance; it is his; he is really and truly said to be rich; but his wealth is in the hands of his guardian who holds it in trust for him. His guardian imparts to him as he needs during his minority. It is only when he reaches full manhood that he enters on the enjoyment of his estate. During the years of his non-age, he trusts his guardian for the supply of his daily wants, and applies to him for it. So the believer already possesses the inheritance in Christ; complete salvation is already his; while in this world he trusts in him for the supply of his continually returning wants, and applies to him for it, but when the appointed time arrives, he enters on the full enjoyment of the inheritance.

Receiving and resting in Christ for salvation, as he is offered in the gospel, we begin to live holy lives, seeking to walk in all the commandments and ordinances of the Lord blameless. Let it be noted, that repentance, with all the graces of the Spirit follow from union to Christ. Believers are married to Christ that they may bring forth fruit unto God. "As the branch can not bear fruit of itself except it abide in the vine; no more can ye, except ye abide in me." First one with Christ by faith and the indwelling of his Spirit, and then holy living.

A word to those who are guiding inquirers. The first thing required of the sinner is to go to Christ and believe in him. Beware how you put anything between the sinner and Christ. You may point him to Christ and put the Bible in his hands; you may take him to the Bible-class, the Sabbath-school, the prayer-meeting and the church, to help him to Christ, but beware that you do not lead him to trust Bible, or church, or prayer-meeting, or Sabbath-school, or teacher, or minister, instead of Christ. Remove every obstacle out of his way; help him to Christ at once; seek to make him intimate with him. Salvation is in Christ; a full, a free, a present salvation, for every soul of man that believeth; and the sinner will find it nowhere else in all the universe of God. Let your cry constantly be, "Behold the Lamb of God which taketh away the sin of the world."

ASSURANCE OF SALVATION.

DEAR FRIEND.—In your letter of the 11th inst., you refer to mine of the 17th of September, in which I pressed on young ministers the importance of being assured of their interests in Christ and final salvation that they might successfully guide others. You say " I do not possess the assurance," and you ask me to explain more particularly how it may be obtained. With this request I cheerfully comply. It is a terrible thing to live in constant fear of wrath, never to taste the blessedness of sins forgiven and to know nothing of peace with God. In this state one can make but little growth in grace, and render but unsatisfactory service to his Master. Certainly this " confidence hath great recompense of reward," and'should be sought with all diligence. There is, however, a preliminary question which demands attention: " Is this assurance attainable?" I believe that it is, not only as an occasional enjoyment, but also as a habitual state. I believe that it is our privilege to live in the fruition of the peace that passeth all understanding. However, before pointing out what I believe to be " God's way of peace," I desire to call your attention to some considerations in confirmation of this position:

The Scriptures seem to me to proceed on the sup-
position that the believers of the primitive church
did maintain this assurance; not merely eminent
saints such as Job, David, Isaiah and the Apostles,
but the men and women generally of the churches
to which the epistles were directed. First, I ask
you to notice some general declarations of the Word
of God.

In the epistle to the Romans i: 6, 7. Paul uses the
following language: "Among whom are ye also
the called of Jesus Christ, beloved of God, called to
be saints." He speaks as though there was no doubt
about this calling and saintship. In chap. v: 1–5,
he addresses the Romans as persons being
justified, having peace with God. access, rejoicing
in hope of the glory of God, and as glorying in
tribulations also. Their assurance seems to be
implied in every line of these verses. In the eighth
chapter, 15–18, the same fact is implied. "For ye
have not received the spirit of bondage again to fear:
but ye have received the spirit of adoption whereby
we cry, Abba, Father, The Spirit also beareth witness with our spirit that we are the children of
God. * * For I reckon that the sufferings
of this present time are not worthy to be compared
with the glory which shall be revealed in us." The
whole of this chapter, you will observe, is in the
same strain. In addition to these scriptures,

examine II Cor. v: 1-21; Col. i: 12, 13; I Peter i:
8, 9; I John, iii: 2; Rev. i: 5, 6. I refer to these
texts simply as specimens. To quote all that imply
the assurance of believers would be to quote whole
chapters and epistles. Indeed every word addressed
to those called "saints" seems to imply this great
fact.

I ask your attention also to the fact that many
of the richest and most precious promises are
addressed to the assured. Take for example,
Romans viii: 28, "And we know that all things
work together for good to them that love God, to
them who are the called according to his purpose."
You must know that you love God and that you are
called according to His purpose before you can say,
"All things shall work toge' 'er for my good."
Again, turn to the epistle to ... Ephesians; read
over the first three chapters carefully. How exalted
the positions in which the "saints and the faithful"
are there represented as standing! How bright and
glorious the future opening before them! and yet,
before you can comfort yourself with these words,
you must know yourself to be a saint and to be
faithful in Christ Jesus. Of the same tenor are the
two epistles that follow, and many of the Psalms.
As a specimen of the latter, study carefully the 4th
and 91st. Before we can feed on these rich and
precious promises, we must know ourselves to be
among those to whom they are addressed.

There is another fact worthy of special attention in this connection: the strongest motives which the apostles addressed to believers, when exhorting them to lives of holiness, are applicable only to the assured. Notice the following: I Cor. vi: 20, "For ye are bought with a price, therefore glorify God in your body and in your spirit, which are God's." I Cor. xv: 58, "Therefore, my beloved brethren, be ye steadfast, unmovable, always abounding in the work of the Lord, forasmuch as ye know that your labor is not in vain in the Lord." Ephesians iv: 32, "And be ye kind to one another, tender-hearted, forgiving one another, even as God for Christ's sake hath forgiven you." I John ii: 12, 13, 14, 15, "I write unto you, little children, because your sins are forgiven you for his name's sake. * * * Love not the world, neither the things that are in the world."

In addition to all this, we have many earnest exhortations to maintain this assurance. See I Peter, i: 10; Heb. vi: 10, 11; x: 22, 34.

These considerations, I think, show that an assurance of salvation is attainable: that it should be habitually maintained; that in it we may find unspeakable happiness, and that it is necessary in order that we may go up to the highest plane of Christian standing, attain to the holiest living, and to the most devoted service.

The question now arises, How is this peace or

assurance which we have seen to have been the common possession of primitive Christians to be attained? To the answer to this question I now ask your attention. It is a fact that the Scriptures connect peace or assurance with faith or trust, intimately and immediately. John xiv: 1, " Let not your heart be troubled; ye believe in God, believe also in me." Our Lord here prescribes for a troubled heart. His direction is, " Believe in me." We are, hence, certainly warranted in believing that faith in Christ will remove trouble from the heart and bring peace. Romans v: 1. " Therefore being justified by faith, we have peace with God through our Lord Jesus Christ." Peace follows immediately on being justified by faith. The verses that follow imply the attainment of assurance at the very beginning of the Christian course. Romans xv: 13. " Now the God of hope fill you with all joy and peace in believing." Here you will observe it is *peace in believing*. I Peter i: 8, 9. " Whom having not seen ye love; in whom, though now ye see him not, yet believing, ye rejoice with joy unspeakable and full of glory; receiving the end of your faith, even the salvation of your souls." Here joy and rejoicing, which certainly imply a peaceful assurance, are represented as growing immediately out of faith. In Acts xvi: 34, it is said that the jailer " rejoiced, believing in God with all his house." Isaiah xxvii: 3, " Thou wilt keep

him in perfect peace. whose mind is stayed on thee.
because he trusteth in thee." Here peace is connected intimately with trust. These scriptures are
but specimens. They teach fully and clearly an
Assurance of Faith.

The question now arises, How does faith or trust
bring peace? There are three difficulties in the way
of peace, any one or all of which may keep the mind
in a state of unrest, and prevent that calm assurance which we desire. all of which are removed by
faith.

1. "Is God disposed to love? Is he merciful?"
I answer, the Scriptures testify abundantly on this
subject. "God is love." "His mercies are great:
his tender mercies are over all his works. He is
good and ready to forgive, and plenteous in mercy
unto all that call upon him." "Herein is love, not
that we loved God. but that he loved us and gave
his son to be the propitiation of our sins." Acquaint
thyself with God and have peace. Now. if you
believe these things concerning God, you can have
no trouble because God is not merciful. Faith
removes out of the way all obstacles to peace coming
from this source.

2. "But God is just as well as merciful. He
must save men justly or not at all. Can he justly
save a sinner?" I answer. Consider Christ's finished
work. He undertook for us. upon him were laid the

iniquities of us all, he was obedient unto death, he bare our sins in his own body on the tree. The Son has thus satisfied the demands of law and justice, so that now God can be just and justify him which believeth in Jesus. God can righteously pardon; more, he cannot righteously condemn a single believer. Now, if you believe this great truth, another obstacle in the way of peace is removed. There is no reason whatever, why trouble should come from this source. Faith in Christ's finished work removes it all.

3. But a third difficulty still remains: "What right have I to believe that God is willing to save me? What is my warrant for believing in his Son for salvation? I answer, God has given, granted, tendered to you a full and free salvation in Christ, and expressly warranted you to trust in him for it. John iii: 16, "God so loved the world that he gave his only begotten Son that whosoever believeth in him should not perish, but have everlasting life." I John v: 11, "And this is the record, that God hath given us eternal life, and this life is in his Son." Rev. xxii: 17, "And whosoever will, let him take the water of life freely." 2d Cor. ix: 15, "Thanks be unto God for his unspeakable gift."

The Scriptures are full of similar statements. God has granted, given, tendered Christ to sinners, to you and me as a Saviour, and in him a complete

salvation. Now what is to be done about it? I
answer, (1.) Believe this glorious record of the
mercy of God, of the work of Christ and the free
grant of salvation in him. (2). Take the gift thus
freely given, and remember the moment you receive
Christ as your Saviour, your Prophet, Priest and
King, his salvation in all its fulness becomes yours,
you are complete in him. (3.) Trust in Christ,
according to the warrant so plainly given, to impart
to you this salvation as you need it. Now, if you
thus believe the record, thus accept the gift, and
thus rest in Christ for salvation as he is offered in
the gospel, where will your trouble be? Will it
not have vanished? Will you not be at peace,
resting in the Lord for salvation? And will not
this peace come from looking unto Jesus, and not
to yourself? Analyze "trust." It involves three
elements—(1.) A person trusting. (2.) A person
trusted. (3.) A thing trusted for. But trust for a
thing means expectation of that thing. You have
money in the bank; you trust in the bank to pay
you that money on demand; you expect it and are at
rest about it because you have faith in the bank.
You have salvation in Christ. God has given you
Christ, and assured you that there is a life in him
for you. You trust in him for it, and expect it
through him, why not be at rest about it? Apply
to him and you will receive according to your need,

11

for it is written, Phil. iv: 19, "But my God shall supply all your need according to his riches in glory by Christ Jesus." In 1856, I received a document signed by James Thompson, Secretary of the Board of Trustees of Monmouth College, tendering me the Presidency of that institution and promising me on condition of acceptance, a specific salary. I believed that document to be genuine, I accepted the tender therein made. Though still in Boston, I believed that I had been called to become President of that College; I trusted in the Trustees to put me in possession of all the rights and privileges pertaining to that office, and pay me the promised salary. I was at peace about these matters. I had full assurance on the subject, and all because I had faith in certain men, and that, too, before I had exercised a single prerogative of the office, or touched a dollar. That faith brought me to Monmouth, and the constant verification of my expectations but strengthened the faith which I had at the beginning. So God has tendered you in Christ forgiveness, acceptance, life, saintship, sonship and kingship. You believe that the tender has been made; you accept the gift offered, and now believing the truth of what God has told you, you believe yourself to be forgiven, accepted, to have eternal life, to be a saint, a son, a king, and all this before you begin to enjoy the rights and privileges of your new relationship.

Moreover, you trust in Christ to do for you according to the promise. Thus you may be at peace, and rest in the Lord in full confidence of salvation before you even raise the question of your interest in Christ, or begin to inquire as to your state. This assurance we call assurance of faith. It is attained simply by believing in him. It comes at the beginning of our course. It enables one to rejoice in the Lord at once, and to enter on holy living and loving service in the full enjoyment of the liberty of the sons of God before we begin to inquire after evidences that we are children of God at all. Assurance of faith precedes assurance of sense. In my next. I shall have something to say about this latter kind of assurance. In the meantime permit me to recommend to your careful study, "Erskine on Faith and Assurance of Faith," "Anderson on Faith," and "God's way of Peace"—a most valuable little book from the pen of Dr. Bonar, of Edinburgh. The first named, you may find in E. Erskine's sermons. His sermons on this subject have been published by the A. T. S. in a separate volume. I am sorry to say that "Anderson" is out of print. It is to be hoped that our Board of Publication will soon issue a new edition of it. We ought not to permit such valuable works to remain inaccessible to our people.

I have called your attention to the " assurance of

faith;" I have now a few things to say about "assurance of sense," as it is commonly called.

The great principles on which this kind of assurance is based are the following: 1. The Spirit of God dwells in every believer, and is working in him to will and to do according to his good pleasure, so that he brings forth the fruits of the Spirit. 2. By our own consciousness, by looking into our own hearts, we may discern the results of this work— results which, in the Word of God, we have a warrant to expect. These are commonly called the marks of a child of God, evidences of saving faith. 3. Thus we know that we are in Christ by the Spirit which he has given us. These evidences are fully delineated in the first epistle of John. A careful study of that epistle will, I am persuaded, bring one to a full knowledge of the distinguishing characteristics of the sons of God. 4. From Phil. i: 6, we are assured that "he which hath begun a good work in you will perform it." Here we find the grand old doctrine of the perseverance of the saints to be one of the main pillars of this assurance. 5. From these premises we may be assured of our final salvation. The method is simply this: He that believeth shall be saved; I believe, therefore I shall be saved. As numerous and various as are the marks by which the sons of God are distinguished, so numerous and various are the minor premises of this syllogism. The difficulty consists in determining whether or no we possess these marks. Because of the remains within us of indwelling sin, and of its continuous activity, lusting against the Spirit, in some cases it becomes so difficult to settle this great question that, were there no other method of assurance, we might, as many do, live in doubt all our days.

Comparing and contrasting assurance of faith and assurance of sense, we shall better understand the nature of both. The first comes with the first exercise of faith, and may be very strong at the beginning; the other comes after the fulfillment of the promise as realized in our own experience, and becomes fuller and clearer as the fruits of the Spirit are produced in us more abundantly. The one is direct; the other reflex. The one has its object without, we find it in the Word; the other within, we find it in our own experience. Faith looks to the veracity of the promiser; sense to the fulfillment of the promise. Noah, trusting in the declaration of God, was assured of his safety before the flood came. This was assurance of faith. When the Ark rested securely on Ararat he had assurance of sense. Faith looks to the future good promised; sense, to the present good received.

These two kinds of assurance mutually strengthen and help each other. You examine the grant made of Christ to sinners as recorded in the gospel. You inspect carefully the warrant which the sinner had to believe. You perceive that you have a full and complete warrant to receive Christ as your Saviour, and trust in him to impart to you out of his fulness grace for grace. You do thus receive and rest in him, and exclaim, "Jesus is mine and I am his." You now begin to note the "MY'S" of the Psalms, and rejoice in their wonderful richness. You trust in him according to the word of promise which he has given you. You rejoice and are exceeding glad. You walk at liberty. In time you find the promises are being fulfilled in your own experience. Thus your faith is strengthened, and the assurance which it brings made, if possible. doubly sure. The surer you are of your interest in Christ, the fuller will be your love, the deeper your penitence, and more earnest your devotion. Thus you will go on from strength to strength unweariedly. You will live a holy life; you will render a free, happy, joyous service. Your service will be neither that of hireling nor that of a slave, but that of a son conscious of his son-ship. But in all this, other foundation must no man lay than that which is laid—Jesus Christ the righteous. We must beware how we put frames, feelings, experiences in place of Christ. If we do, our confidence will be as fitful as the wind. That it may be abiding, it must rest in that which abides.

At first I had no adequate understanding of the assurance of faith. I was constantly looking for assurance of sense. Sometimes I was elevated, sometimes depressed. I lived and ministered in a sadly troubled state. At length I made known my state of mind to Dr. McCarrol—an eminent saint— and to another distinguished servant of God still living. They led me into a department of thought at that time almost entirely new to me. I read and studied Anderson, Erskine, Marshall, and Hervey. My eyes were opened. I began to see light clearly. I became a free man. And since that time, I thank God, I have been kept in the enjoyment of singu- larly uniform peace, trusting in the Lord. In avowing this I do not exalt myself, but the faithful- ness of a covenant keeping God and Saviour. The same way is open to you; and my heart's desire and · prayer to God is, that you and all the brethren may possess the peace that passeth understanding, and may run with patience the race that is set before us, looking into Jesus the author and finisher of our faith.

THE HOLY SPIRIT.

I. The indwelling of the Spirit. "What, know ye not that your body is the temple of the Holy Ghost, which is in you which ye have of God?" "Know ye not that ye are the temple of God, and that the Spirit of God dwelleth in you?" "For ye are the temple of the living God; as God hath said. I will dwell in them and walk in them." "In whom all the building, fitly framed together, groweth into a holy temple in the Lord; in whom ye also are builded together for a habitation of God through the Spirit." "The Spirit of him that raised up Jesus from the dead shall dwell in you." "And hereby we know that he abideth in us by the Spirit which he hath given to us." The great truth here taught is obvious: The Holy Spirit dwelleth in every believer. whether young or old, of strong or weak faith, of large attainments or small, the believer is a temple of the Holy Ghost. The indwelling of the Spirit is not a promised blessing; it is the present possession of all those who believe.

The "indwelling spirit" is the "comforter" promised by our Lord. The term "comforter," or "paraclete," denotes one who lays hold with us to help us in bearing a heavy burden, in performing a difficult task. I will pray the Father, and he will give you another comforter, that he may abide with you forever; even the Spirit of truth, whom the world cannot receive, because it seeth him not. neither knoweth him: but ye know him, for he dwelleth in you, and shall be in you.' "But the comforter, which is the Holy Ghost, whom the Father will send in my name, he shall teach you all things and bring all things to your remembrance, whatsoever I have said unto you." " But when the comforter is come, whom I will send unto you from the Father, even the spirit of truth, * * * he shall testify of me." " It is expedient for you that I go away; for, if I go not away, the comforter will not come unto you, but if I depart I will send him unto you. And when he is come, he will reprove the world of sin, and of righteousness and of judgment." " Howbeit when he, the spirit of truth, is come, he will guide you into all truth; for he will not speak of himself, but whatsoever he shall hear that shall he speak. and he will show you things to come. He shall glorify me, for he shall receive of mine and show it unto you." To what dignity has he advanced us in making us temples of his Spirit! What a glorious privilege to be blessed and honored by such a guest dwelling in us!

II. What evidence may any one have that the Holy Spirit dwells in him. The following is to me satisfactory:

The Holy Spirit is given to every believer. "This spake he of the Spirit which they that believe on him should receive."

The Holy Spirit is given to them who truly repent. " Repent and be baptized every one of you in the name of Jesus Christ, for the remission of sins, and ye shall receive the gift of the Holy Ghost."

The Holy Spirit is given to all the children of God: " For as many as are led by the Spirit of God they are the sons of God. For ye have not received the spirit of bondage again to fear; but ye have received the spirit of adoption, whereby we cry Abba, Father. The Spirit itself beareth witness with our spirit, that we are the children of God." And because ye are sons, God hath sent forth the Spirit of his Son into your hearts."

The Holy Spirit is given to all the people of God: " Now, if any man have not the Spirit of Christ, he is none of his."

The Holy Spirit is given to all those who are in Christ, and who have received Christ into their hearts: " He that keepeth his commandments dwelleth in him and he in him. And hereby we know that he abideth in us, by the Spirit which he hath given us."

Now, whatever evidence any one has that he believes on the Lord Jesus Christ, has repented and turned unto the Lord, is a child of God, is one of

God's people, or that he is in Christ, or Christ is in him, is also evidence that he is a temple of the Holy Spirit. The whole range of evidence of our interest in Christ, is evidence that the Holy Ghost dwelleth in us. Have you received the Lord Jesus? Do you believe on his name? Have you repented of your sins? Are you Christ's and is he your Saviour? Are you one of his children? Then the Holy Ghost dwelleth in you.

But "the fruits of the Spirit are love, joy, peace, long suffering, gentleness, goodness, faith, meekness, temperance." The Holy Ghost that dwelleth in us is bringing forth these fruits. As by examining the fruit that grows on a tree you determine its character, so by examining the fruits, which you are bringing forth, you may learn whether or no the heavenly guest is abiding in you. In applying this test, two things should, however, be kept in mind. First, The question is not, are these fruits being produced in great abundance and perfection, but do they exist at all in any quantity or of any quality? It is not, do you love God with your whole heart, soul, mind and strength, but do you love him at all? It is not, is your soul filled with joy in the Lord; but does this grace exist at all? It is not, have you a triumphant faith, without a shadow of doubt or misgiving; but do you believe at all? The same principle applies to the other fruits enumerated. If they have been produced to any degree, then the Spirit is in you, for these are the fruits of the Spirit.

Another fact should never be forgotten. Indwelling sin is not completely extirpated from the hearts of the children of God during their wanderings and warfare in the wilderness. A new man has been created in every one of them, but the old man remains and acts. The house of David has been set up, but the house of Saul has not been utterly destroyed, it still claims authority and seeks to establish it. The child of God "delights in his law after the inward man, but he sees another law in his members warring against the law of his mind, and bringing him into captivity to the law of sin which is in his members. The flesh lusteth against the spirit and the spirit against the flesh, and these are contrary the one to the other, so that ye cannot do the things that ye would." You go into your orchard; you find there weeds, thorns and briers; but you do not conclude that there can therefore be no apple, or pear, or peach trees in it. You often find very excellent fruit in great abundance, in a very poorly kept orchard. You examine your heart; you ought not to conclude that there can be no love, or joy, or faith in it, nor any of the fruits of the Spirit, because you find that the lusts of the flesh have not all been rooted out. It is the office and work of the Spirit to mortify these lusts, and one day they shall disappear and not one be left remaining. Over the body of this death you shall gain the victory through our Lord Jesus Christ. Of his fullness, shall all we receive, even grace for grace, until we are made perfect in holiness.

Bearing these two facts in mind, you may, from the fruits which you bear, know assuredly that the Holy Ghost dwelleth in you.

But you answer, "I don't know. I am not sure, I am still in doubt." If this is so, then, "Behold the Lamb of God, that taketh away the sin of the world." Remember his finished work, the infinite worth of his atonement, and the wonderous love from which it proceeded. Receive Christ as yours. Trust in him according to the promise. Repent of your sins and turn unto the Lord with all your heart, and you have the guarantee of a covenant keeping God that, at once the Spirit shall be given you, and you will become a "habitation of God through the Spirit."

III. How may the believer distinguish the leadings and teachings of the Spirit, from other thoughts and feelings? The writer does not profess to be able to answer this question fully and satisfactorily: his aim is only to help inquirers in their investigations. The attention of students of the Word of God is respectfully invited to the following principles:

1. The Holy Spirit never leads the believer to

accept as true or right anything contrary to the Word of God. His teachings are not self-contradictory. What he speaks in the heart always agrees with the written word. Whatever, therefore, is clearly inconsistent with that word is not of the Spirit. But the Holy Spirit dwells in the believer as a Spirit of wisdom and revelation in the knowledge of Christ, and we have a clear warrant to trust in him to enlighten the eyes of our understanding, that we may know what is the hope of his calling and what the riches of the glory of his inheritance in the saints, and what the exceeding greatness of his power to usward who believe. While therefore his teachings always accord with the written word, he helps us to understand better its meaning, and to feel more fully its power.

2. The Holy Spirit never leads the believer to exercise, or excites within him, the lusts of the flesh enumerated in Galatians v: 19, 21. He does however excite and strengthen the graces named in the following verses. Anything, therefore, that tends to "idolatry, witchcraft, hatred, variance, emulations, wrath, strife, seditions, heresies, envyings, murders, drunkenness, revellings and such like," are not of the Spirit. But "love, joy, peace, long suffering, gentleness, goodness, faith, meekness and temperance," in the sense of the apostle always are.

3. The Holy Spirit never leads us to believe any-

thing which sound reason legitimately exercised condemns as untrue; or to crush out natural affections when exercised within just limits, or to do anything condemned by an enlightened conscience. He does not lead men to believe that two and two are ten, or that parallel lines meet, or that a circle is a square; he does not teach us that love of children, or of parents, or of brothers and sisters, or of friends, or of country is wrong: he does not teach that falsehood, or theft, or murder is right. But at the same time the Spirit strengthens the understanding so that it may perceive the truth more clearly, and be kept from error; represses natural affection when exercised beyond just limits, and rectifies and enlightens the conscience, so that it may not approve and move men to do that which is wrong.

4. The Holy Spirit glorifies Christ because he takes the things of Christ and shows them unto the believer. He exhibits the Saviour as pre-eminently trustworthy, setting forth the wondrous love manifested in him, his finished work and willingness to save to the very uttermost, and thus strengthens the faith of the believer. He inflames his love by exhibiting him as the chief among ten thousand and altogether lovely, and as full of loving kindness and tender mercy. He also sets forth our Saviour as rightful King and Lord, and thus leads us to submission and obedience. By manifold exhibitions of

Christ he strengthens many graces, and brings forth these graces in his people more abundantly. Low thoughts of Christ are not of the Spirit; high, commonly are.

5. When we feel the need of help and look to God for Christ's sake by his Spirit to minister to us as we need, and with absolute submission to his teachings and leadings wait on him, we have a good and sufficient warrant to trust in him that in the time of need he will help us as we need, making plain to us the truth, showing us what is right and pointing out the way that is wisest and best. David prays: " Show me thy ways, O Lord; teach me thy paths. Lead me in thy truth and teach me; for thou art the God of my salvation, on thee do I wait all the day." He assigns as a reason for praying thus: " Good and upright is the Lord; therefore will he teach sin- ners in the way. The meek will he guide in judgment, the meek will he teach his way." Again he exhorts: " Commit thy way unto the Lord, trust also in him, and he shall bring it to pass:" " Rest in the Lord and wait patiently for him." For all this he assigns as a reason: " The steps of a good man are ordered by the Lord." According to John's testimony, the Comforter, which is the Holy Ghost, whom the Father sends in the name of Christ, is commissioned expressly "to teach us all things." Surely, then, there is no presumption in looking to

and trusting in the Spirit to show us the mind of Christ. Certainly, when we yield to his teachings and leadings with absolute submission, we may depend on him to guide us in judgment and teach us his way. Those who have tried this way have no reason to repent of their conduct. On the contrary, they accept it as one of the highest privileges of God's people thus to be guided by him. But we must beware that we do not condition the Spirit by consenting to accept his teachings only when they agree with our prejudices, and to follow his leadings only when they accord with our wishes. We must also remember that he does not lead us to ignore or reject the written word, or to accept absurdities. We must also remember that he shows us only what is present duty, and not duty at some future time.

In what has been written above, all questions may not have been answered or all difficulties removed. Hints, however, I trust have been given which they will find helpful who desire to live in the Spirit. Those who long to know the mind of Christ, desire it above all other knowledge, and are accustomed to listen for the voice of his Spirit and wait to be taught by him, will not find it difficult to distinguish his voice and his teachings. We soon learn to know the voice and the sentiments of those with whom we dwell. We do not find it difficult to tell the footfall of an intimate acquaintance, even at a distance. Surely, surely, then, God's people, with whom and in whom the Holy Ghost constantly dwells, may learn without difficulty to distinguish his voice, and need never mistake it for that of a stranger.

IV. "I am a believer on the Lord Jesus Christ. According to the testimony of God, the Holy Ghost dwelleth in me. What then?"

1. Be thankful for this great gift. When your Saviour left this world he could not make up the loss to his disciples in any way more effectually than by sending his Spirit to abide with them and to be in each of them. That Spirit is in you. as a Spirit of grace and supplication, as a Spirit of wisdom and revelation in the knowledge of Christ, as a Spirit of holiness, as a Spirit of adoption, and as a Spirit of promise. It is leading and guiding you, and is bringing forth in you the most precious fruits. Your Lord by his Spirit is doing great things for you. Rejoice therefore and be glad, and give vent to your joy in words of praise and thanksgiving.

2. Grieve not the Holy Spirit of God whereby ye are sealed unto the day of redemption. Remember that he has taken up his abode with you and will remain with you a permanent guest, than whom you can have none of greater dignity. Now if you permit your heart to be filled with thoughts and aspirations with which the Spirit of God can have no sympathy; if you disregard his teachings and

refuse to follow his leadings; if your whole life, internal and external, is of the earth, earthy, you will grieve him and he will cease to a great extent to do his work within you, and your soul will be filled with darkness and doubt, and your life will be without peace or joy, and you will bring forth the fruits of righteousness to a very limited degree indeed. It is a great sin to grieve the Holy Spirit, and you should guard against it with the most watchful care.

3. Study the last eleven verses of the fifth chapter of the epistle to the Galatians. Here believers are represented as being led by the Spirit, and are exhorted to walk in the Spirit and live in the Spirit. To this end we must accept the truths which our Lord teaches by his word and Spirit; we must not do the works of the flesh but bring forth the fruits of the Spirit, we must follow the leadings of the Spirit in all holy living and devoted service. Living thus, we walk in the light and are at liberty. The life which we live will be a holy life, a life of faith, of peace and joy, we go on rejoicing in the Lord. This is the only life which as Christian men and women we should be content to live.

4. Pray for the Spirit. "If ye then being evil know how to give good gifts to your children, how much more will your heavenly Father give the Holy Spirit to them that ask him." True you may not

pray for the Spirit in the same sense, that those to whom these words were originally addressed could; for the Holy Ghost was not then given, because the Son was not yet glorified, while the Spirit already dwelleth in you. Still you can pray God for Christ's sake that the Spirit that dwelleth in you may manifest himself by bringing forth in you much fruit; you can pray that the Holy Spirit may come in power on the world that lieth in sin, rendering the word effectual and reproving the world of sin, of righteousness and of judgment, and you can also pray that the Spirit may come and dwell in the hearts of those who have him not and who are strangers to his presence and power. Fail not to honor the Spirit by duly appreciating his work and seeking his precious influences.

5. To the end that you may discharge fully the obligations resting on you towards the Spirit, study the doctrine of the Spirit carefully and do what in you lies to comprehend it fully.

THE STATE AND TEMPERANCE.

A lecture delivered in the United Presbyterian Church, at Wooster, Ohio, in the winter of 1882–3.

The question coming to the front just now is not, Is intemperance an evil, and should men be temperate? Not, Is it our duty to persuade men from drinking and to become abstainers? But, Has the State anything to do with it as to the manufacture and sale of alcohol? As a drug for use in medicine and the arts, there is no question. The difference relates altogether to the manufacture and sale of intoxicating liquors as a beverage. The question is not, What is the platform of this party or that? The question is not, What does the constitution of the country say? The question is not, What is public opinion on the subject? But, What does God's law of righteousness demand of the nation and Government in relation to this evil, acknowledged to be very great? Some maintain that the State can do nothing.

They say every man has a right to make money in this way if he choose; every man has a right to drink or get drunk if he choose, and it is nobody's business but his own. Liberty is the individual right of every man, and the State has no right to

(181)

interfere with a man, no right to tell him that he
shall not follow this or that business. The State
has no right to meddle with what people eat or
drink. Its duty is to let this matter alone. Liberty
is the inalienable right of every man. But liberty
has its limitations. No man has a right to do
wrong. No man has a right to steal. No man has
a right to adulterate his goods and sell them as
pure. No man has a right to establish a slaughter-
house or a glue factory in the center of Wooster.
No man has a right to buy a lot down town and then
plant on it a powder factory. Why is this? you
ask. If he sees fit to invest his money in such a
business and carry it on in that place, who has a
right to interfere? The answer is, by establishing
any such business he interferes with the rights of
his neighbors. That is the simple principle. Now.
no man has a right to do anything that interferes
with the rights of others. All have equal rights
before God and before just government. No man
has a right, therefore, to lift up his little finger in
performing an act that will be a trespass upon the
rights of others. In the broad domain which lies
outside of the rights of others, as far as they are
concerned, he has perfect liberty; but across it he
may not go. This is fundamental. This is recognized in all books on government, by all writers on
this great subject of natural rights. You and I and

every man, therefore, must use our liberty so as not to trespass. Remember that.

And this brings up my first principal point: Does the traffic in intoxicating drinks trespass on any man's rights? This is the great fundamental question. Is this a business in which men may engage and meddle with no right which another man or woman possesses? If it is, then Government may say to him no word of prohibition. If it is not, then Government has the same right to interfere that it has to interfere in another business, which in itself or in the method of its management, trespasses upon the rights of others.

And, first, every man has a right to as pure and lofty moral character as he can attain and maintain —to be as pure, sober and honest as possible. Is not that so? Have you not a right to become as virtuous as you can? Nobody will deny that. And no one has a right to interfere with you, to hinder you in getting up to higher attainments in virtue. No man has a right to place a straw in your way as a stumbling block when you are endeavoring to become purer and better. And much more, no man has a right to lay a hand on you and pull you down. If a man goes into a farmer's field and takes away a lamb or pig, not worth a dollar, he trespasses upon that man's rights, and the law will summon its officers, and will send them forth to hunt, far and near, until that piece of property is found and restored, though the cost of the work be ten times the value of the property taken away. It was the duty of the State to protect that man in his right to that piece of property. Here is the right to character. Is any man at liberty to trespass there? Is it a trifling thing, demanding no attention from the State, if the other is sufficient to warrant its interference? Look at the intemperate man. You go to him and tell him of his sin and danger. His eyes are opened. He sees it and determines to reform. He will promise you he will never drink again. Yes, he will lift up his right hand and swear before Almighty God that he will never drink again. Yes, he will puncture his veins, dip his pen into the blood, and write down the oath that he will never drink again. He goes forth in the strength of his solemn purpose. Now, has any man a right to tempt that man to drink? Has he not the right to walk the streets in safety? Is not that so? But at every corner he meets the tempter. The open saloon, the significant signs, and the suggestive odor, all tempt him. He hesitates, he yields, he enters, he drinks, he falls. Is there not a trespass in such a case? I ask, is that man who goes forth from his home in all the strength of a high and holy purpose to endeavor to walk in the ways of righteousness to be protected? Has he no rights?

Do the men who tempt him not commit a trespass? What is the stealing of a bit of property, worth a dollar or two, as a trespass compared with that by which temptation has been put in his path that has led him to fall?

In the second place, the wife and mother and children have rights that need protection. They are dependent upon the husband and father for support, for clothing, for shelter and education. Their all is invested in the father. Their all depends upon his sobriety, his diligence, his honesty. The intemperate man can support and take care of his children but imperfectly. Every glass he drinks diminishes his ability to support them, secure them education, and give them proper care. He becomes a drunkard, and his ability to care for his wife and children is absolutely destroyed. But for the men who sell he might have been sober. He resolves, he promises, he is tempted, and falls. If the tempter did not meet him on every corner he might stand. Has there been no trespass upon the rights of that wife and mother and of those children? Have they no right to protection? Suppose a man breaks into the yard and leads away the cow upon which these children depend for their daily subsistence. Information is given to the officers, and they go forth and hunt him down, and spend large money in doing it. Why such trouble and cost? Ah, there has been a trespass upon the rights of that mother and children. And they talk about the little ones starving at home. But has there been no trespass when that man was tempted and fell, and their resources utterly dried up?

In the third place, it is the duty of parents to train up their children in the nurture and admonition of the Lord: so to train them that they may be sober, upright, honest men and women, and good citizens. It is their duty, and if they do not do it we are swift in finding fault with them. And they have a right to do this. They have a right to be left free to do it without let or hindrance. No man has a right to interfere with those parents or make their duty difficult. But the seller of intoxicating drink tempts the boys, suggests the gratification of appetite, and makes it easy, Because of the open saloon the boys of the land learn to drink, become drunkards and are ruined. Without them they might have been sober, honest, upright children; boys that would do honor to a father and mother; men that would have been a blessing to the Church and the world. But now what are they? Rotten carcasses. You as a father may lavish tender care; you may lavish days and nights of toil upon your children: you may spend and are spent for their welfare. You do the best you can to train them. You instill into them lessons of truth, righteousness and temperance.

They grow up. They go out. They see the open
saloons. They ask what is inside of those blinds.
They go at first from curiosity. They see the shining bottles. They smell the drink. They are
tempted to taste. They learn to love it, and in spite
of all the care of home down they go to ruin. Many,
many a family has been draped in mourning through
this process. But for the open saloon this might
not have occurred. Now, my friends, is it the duty
of parents to bring up their children to be sober
men? Have they not the right to be permitted to
do it? Has any man on earth a right to interfere,
to make it difficult or impossible for them to do it?
And whenever there is such interference is there not
a trespass? Better a thousand times sweep away a
man's estate and leave him penniless than sweep
away the character of his sons and leave them des-
pised drunkards. Welcome a thousand times a home
in yonder infirmary than come to such an end.

In the fourth place, the State has a right to tax
citizens so as to raise the money needful for the
work of government. But it may not rightfully add
one cent more. It is usurpation. The State has a
right to demand a moderate tax as the needs of the
government may require. No man has a right to
pursue any vocation that will needlessly increase
the expense of the government and cause higher
taxes.

Now, concerning the liquor traffic this is true. I cannot amplify these points, I simply state them, after careful investigation, believing that they are within the truth. It is true, first, that it causes an annual waste of about $600,000,000. As a consequence there is that much less taxable property, and of course the remainder must pay higher taxes.

Again, it causes a diminution of production. Drinking men and drunkards produce less than sober men; hence there is less taxable property, less property on which to raise taxes, because of nonproduction, and because of the waste of drinking.

Not only this, but it is the cause of at least three-fourths of the pauperism. Statistics which I have place it at eighty or ninety per cent. And, since it is the cause of three-fourths of the pauperism, therefore the taxes necessary to support three-fourths of the paupers must be added to the cost of the traffic.

It is also the cause of at least three-fourths of the crime. Some statistics make it as high as ninety-nine per cent. I have made a moderate estimate of it. Now, the expense of this must be added to the taxation. No man has a right to pursue any business which thus diminishes the taxable property and adds to the taxes which must be annually levied. Citizens may lawfully complain of all the taxes they are compelled to pay because of the manufacture and

sale of intoxicating drinks. They may complain of
it as a grievance demanding redress and protection.
The public has a right to health. No man has a
right to pursue any business that will unnecessarily
injure the healthfulness of any community and produce disease. The government acts constantly upon
this principle. No man would be permitted to engage
in any business in any community which would be
prejudicial to life or health in that community.
But drinking and drunkenness are prejudicial to
the public health. Now I desire to give you some
evidence on that point, for it is one to which attention is not usually called. This is from a statement
recently published, of a distinguished jurist, an
Associate Justice of the Superior Court of Massachusetts. This is not from a clergyman.

"In considering the relation of alcohol to the public health, we are not to confine ourselves to its
effects upon its immediate victims, but to look at its
effects upon the sanitary condition of the community
and its tendency to produce a propagating *nidus* of
disease. And here, first, we notice that poverty, of
which drink is the principal cause. especially in our
large cities, is one of the prime factors of all disease.
It is this poverty, hopeless and degrading, which
compels its victims to huddle together in tenement
houses, where the decencies of life are not possible.
and where the malignant influences of the external

situation are reinforced by the pestiferous influences within. When to all these is added the lack of clothing for the changes of our climate, the insufficient and unhealthy food, the overwork of mothers, the premature work of children, we can see at once that in such homes as these is the origin and nutriment of malaria and fever; and then it finds for its ready victims the inmates with systems enfeebled and corrupted by debauch and vitiated by hereditary alcoholism.

In New Castle, within a period of two months of the ravages of cholera it struck down one drinker out of fifty-six, of course a far greater proportion of drunkards; only one in 625 of the teetotalers. Throughout the country it always broke out afresh after a festival occasion, and increased after the Sabbath, when the people consumed a little more drink than usual.   Dr. Cartwright, of New Orleans, writes, in 1853, to the Boston *Medical Journal*: "The yellow fever came down like a storm upon this devoted city with 1,127 dram-shops in one of the four parts into which it has been divided.   It is not the citizens proper, but the foreigners, with mistaken notions about the climate and country, who are the chief supporters of these haunts of intemperance. About 5,000 of them died before the epidemic touched a single citizen or sober man, so far as I can get at the facts."

It is upon the last clause we would pause a moment. Five thousand drunkards first—and then? Why, then, the disease, acquiring virulence by feeding upon such material, spreads like a conflagration far and wide, and spares not the noblest and best. It is the cause of introducing disease of the most destructive character, and thus spreading its devastations throughout the community. Now, is not the creation of such hot-beds of disease a trespass? May not the individual claim protection?

Now, my friends, the conclusion that I come to from an examination of these cases, is that the traffic does trespass upon the rights of the man seeking to reform; it does trespass upon the rights of wives of drunkards and drunken men and of their children; it does trespass upon the rights of parents endeavoring to bring up their children in the nurture and admonition of the Lord; it does trespass upon the financial rights of every taxpayer; it does trespass upon the rights of the community to health. The rights of the whole community are invaded in these respects. There is a trespass here. Those men seeking to reform, those wives and mothers, those parents, those taxpayers, the whole people seeking to be free from the contagion of disease, have a right to go before the government, not asking it as a favor merely, but demanding protection. Can there be any question about this? As certainly as any man has a right to go before the government and demand protection against any infringement upon his rights, so certainly has he a right to demand this. And instead, therefore, my friends, of those who are engaged in this business being at liberty to do as they please, and no man meddling with them, the people have a right to demand of them that, as trespassing upon the rights of their neighbors, they shall stop their iniquitous business.

The question comes, then, may the government protect? That is not enough. The government must protect. or it will neglect a most important duty. It is the duty of the government to protect my right to property. It is the duty of the government to protect my liberty, and. in protecting my life. my liberty and property. it does well. But, my friends, what is a man's right to a piece of property compared with a man's right to be sober? What is a woman's right to property compared to her right to have a sober husband? What is the children's right to anything as compared with their right to be free from the curse of a drunken father? What are parents' rights in other respects to compare with their right not to be molested in bringing up their children? What are all the other interferences with the rights of property compared with the enormous taxation to which we are subjected by this traffic? My friends, if it is right to protect the lesser rights, is it not right to protect the greater? Is it not the duty of the government to protect?

But this suggests the third question: Is there any other method than by absolute and complete prohibition? License is wrong in principle and utterly fails to protect the individual. There is no protection in it. There is some regulation and restriction of the traffic and some money made, which goes a little way to meet the expenses which the traffic causes, but as to its protection in other respects there is nothing in it. Taxation protects only in part. But prohibition strikes at the root of the evil. It does protect. But, so far as I can make out, no other method of dealing with it on the part of the State protects at all, except in the case of license taxation.

But here some persons raise an objection. Prohibition, they say, does not prohibit. Men still drink in spite of prohibitory laws. It is ineffective. Well, now, to this I answer, laws against murder, theft and robbery do not suppress these or other crimes. We are constantly reading in the daily papers of murders, and of trespass upon the rights of property, notwithstanding the laws. They do not absolutely abolish the evil, they only diminish trespass upon these rights. Men do not demand the repeal of these laws on the ground that they are inefficient and only diminish the evil instead of abolishing it. And so in respect to the evil under consideration. If the laws diminish the evil it is all that can fairly be demanded of them. It is certainly outrageous to demand that laws prohibitory of the manufacture and sale of intoxicating drinks shall abolish the evil when we do not expect laws against any other evil to do anything more than to diminish it, approximate its abolition. Now the question comes, "Do these laws diminish the evil?" I answer, Yes. The facts prove this beyond controversy.

In 1874, the laws of the State of Illinois rendered it possible for the little city of which I was then a resident [Monmouth] to establish absolute prohibition, and, through the energetic action of half a dozen earnest women, it did it. Every saloon was closed. There was no open saloon in that community. And what was the result? We were told that capital would leave our city; we were told that business would leave us; that the people would not come there to buy or sell; that houses would be hauled off to the prairies for farm dwellings; that grass would grow in the middle of the streets; and then we were told in the same breath, men not noticing the contradiction, that it would do no good, for there would be as much drinking as ever.

Well, what was the result? From that time dated

the prosperity of that city. Business did not leave it. It came to it. The city did not diminish. It increased. Being at the head of a college, I had reason to know something of the difficulties of discipline. Before the close of the saloons one difficulty was from intemperance, from drinking and drunkenness. But after the saloons were closed the difficulty absolutely ceased. It caused us scarce a thought until I left the place. The change from my point of view was most marked. It was said there was as much drinking as ever privately. We went to the agent at the depot, through whose hands every bale of goods must pass, and he testified that the diminution of imports was as great as could be expected.

If any one has doubts on this subject, let him go to our friend Yocum, and hear from the city of Topeka, Kan., a city of 30,000 population, and a large proportion of that class who are most naturally disposed to drink; and yet in that city not an open saloon; not a drunken man to be seen; not a sign of intoxicating drinks anywhere; but all around marks of the greatest prosperity.

Now let me give you the testimony of a distinguished member of the British Parliament, Lord Claude Hamilton, one of the large landed proprietors of Ireland. Now, what can be done in Ireland can be done anywhere: " I am here, as representing the country, to assure you that the facts stated regarding the success of prohibition there are perfectly accurate. There is a district in that country of sixty-one square miles, inhabited by nearly 10.000 people, having three great roads communicating with market towns, in which there are no public houses, entirely owing to the self-action of the inhabitants. The result has been that whereas those high-roads were in former times constant scenes of strife and drunkenness, necessitating the presence of a very considerable number of police to be located in the district, at present there is not a single policeman in that district, the poor-rates are half what they were before, and all the police magistrates testify to the great absence of crime." This is in Ireland, in county Tyrone. Prohibition did diminish crime and pauperism and their evil effects.

Now, another example. It is that of a town in New Jersey, called Vineland. Concerning this town, Pitman, in his "Alcohol and the State," says: "The settlement, from its commencement in 1691, was under the voluntary regime of prohibition, although the law empowering the people to vote on the question of license was not passed till 1863. The vote has always been against license by such overwhelming majorities as to amount to practical unanimity. This city of 10,000 inhabitants, manufacturers, traders, fruit-growers and farmers, spent in 1873 $50 for police, and for the support of the poor only

$400. It would seem from the report of Mr. Curtis, the constable and overseer of the poor for 1874, that there is a slight increase in police expenses, for he says: ' The police expenses of Vineland amount to $75 a year, the sum paid to me.' But a community which has practically no debt, and taxes only 1 per cent. on valuation [Wooster 2 per cent.] can stand this increase well, especially when the constable also reports: 'Though we have a population of 10,000 people, for the period of six months no settler or citizen of Vineland has received relief at my hands as overseer of the poor. Within seventy days there has been only one case, among what we call the floating population, at the expense of $4. During the entire year there has been only one indictment, and that a trifling case of battery among our colored population.'" A poor place for criminal lawyers!

Then the author continues: "This is what prohibition does, be it observed, not for a picked band of religious emigrants, or a community of scholars, but for a miscellaneous company of laborers from all parts of this country, and from Germany, France, England, Ireland and Scotland." Therefore it prohibits effectually in Vineland.

Now, for the very much talked of State of Maine, a State that has tried this as no other State has tried it. Here is the testimony of one of her Governors, who says that:

" The declaration made by many persons that the Maine Law is inoperative, and that liquors are sold freely and in large quantities in this State, is not true. The liquor traffic has been greatly repressed and diminished here and throughout the State, and in many places has been entirely swept away. The law is as well executed generally in this State as other criminal laws are."

Then we have the statement of another Governor, made in 1876:

" Maine has a fixed conclusion on this subject. It is that the sale of intoxicating liquors is an evil of such magnitude that the well-being of the State demands, and the conditions of the social compact warrant, its suppression."

My friends, prohibitory laws may be enforced as well as other criminal laws, and they do protect as well as other laws for the preservation of the rights of the individual.

There is one other objection. They say, " Use moral suasion. You cannot make men virtuous by law; you must use moral suasion." No man thinks of discarding the use of moral suasion, and all the means that can be employed by the Church of the living God to persuade men to be temperate and quit drinking. No man thinks of that. But, my friends, we do not rely exclusively on moral suasion in the case of murder, theft and robbery. There are men who, notwithstanding all you can say, will murder, and we want law to interfere for their punishment, for the punishment of individuals who cannot be reached by moral suasion. True, you cannot make men virtuous by law, but you can do something to compel them to respect the rights of their fellow-men. If they will not love virtue, they may be made to fear the punishment of crime. The duty of government is to protect the welfare of the greatest number. Time will not permit me to go into detail on this point, but you can see at a glance that prohibition, enforced as it is in Topeka, enforced as it is in the little city which I left to come to Wooster, enforced as it is in Vineland, enforced as it is in Maine, enforced as it is even in county Tyrone, Ireland, is a wonderful means of promoting the general welfare. Of this there can be no question.

I might ask your attention to certain minor duties of the State in regard to this subject.

First, as to the drunkard. We have got into the habit of treating him as the poor, unfortunate victim of an evil appetite, and we sympathize with him and coddle him, and make him believe that he is a much-wronged individual. Now, while I believe that the traffic itself is wrong and ought to be dealt with as a trespass upon the rights of men, are we to look upon the individual who drinks and becomes a drunkard, and thus trespasses upon the rights of his wife and children, as innocent? No, my friends; a little law enforced against him might be effective in helping him to stand in his integrity.

In the second place, the officers of the Government should be required to abstain. I say they should be *required* to abstain. Shall the officers of this great nation be drinking men and drunkards? "It is not for kings, O Lemuel, it is not for kings to drink wine, nor for princes strong drink." The habit of using intoxicating drinks should be an absolute disqualification for holding any office, from the lowest to the highest. And instead of the President's being at liberty to load his tables with wines, it should be an impeachable offense.

In the third place, the Government should pay no liquor bills. At least, if our officers and public servants wish to drink, and we choose to allow them, let them pay for it. It is a public disgrace that the Congress of the United States should be called upon to pass appropriations for the liquor bills of men appointed to do honor to the memory of the lamented Garfield. It is enough to make an American citizen blush to think of it. A few years ago I was a member of a committee appointed to visit the Naval Academy at Annapolis. We were accommodated in a government building and supplied with rations by the Government. When I entered that house and was introduced to one of my fellow vis-

itors, his first statement was that in a certain place
I should find free access to all kinds of liquors.
Morning, noon and night there were liquors on the
table, furnished by the Government of the United
States, and paid for out of the revenues of the Government, and the people were taxed to pay for the
liquor used by eleven men out of the twelve who
made up that committee. I say that it is time that
Government liquor bills should be stopped.

Now, what is our duty as men and women? In
the first place, it is our duty to speak out, stand up
and work for temperance. Let us keep men familiar
with the evils of intemperance. Let us keep them
familiar with the dangers of intemperance, the rights
of the people, and the duty of the Government.

In the second place it is our duty to cast our votes
in such a manner as will tell most powerfully in
favor of protection. I do not say that it is our duty
to enter into this organization or that. This is a
question that those who are opposed to the traffic
must settle among themselves; and my counsel to
them would be, "Brethren, see that ye fall not out
by the way." The curse of the cause in many localities is that temperance men are divided, and
their votes have been comparatively powerless.
Whatever may be the policy adopted, it should be
one upon which all can unite. Those who believe
that the rights of the people demand protection
should be united in their vote.

In the next place, it is our duty to do all that we can to enforce existing laws. A distinguished jurist of this city has said that with $1,000 he could close every saloon in the place. Men say the laws cannot be enforced. I know they can be, if the officers of the government and the citizens of the community say they shall be enforced. I have heard that thing said before, but I have seen it proven false. It is only for the people to do their duty, and see to it that the officers do their duty, and the work shall be done. And my word for it, friends, this is the special duty of Christian men. Who shall secure those in their rights, against whom the trespass has been committed, and is being committed, if not God's people? Shall we, servants of Christ, under obligations to stand up and speak out for right everywhere, under obligation everywhere to relieve the distressed, shall we keep silence and leave these men of the world to speak out? No, my friends, it is for us to speak out in clear, unequivocal, unmistakable tones. It is for us to lead the van, calling upon all good men and true to come to our help against the migh'y.

For the sake of the drunkards seeking to reform; for the sake of the wives and children crushed under the curse of a drunken husband and father; for the sake of the parents lying down with aching heads and rising with hearts well-nigh broken, because of sons hastening down to drunkards' graves; for the sake of the young men of our country, so many of whom are being dragged down into the vortex of perdition; for the sake of the nation we love so well, and for which, in the past, many have done so much; and for the sake of Him, the habitation of whose throne is judgment and justice; for the sake of Him who has loved us and given Himself for us, let us do all that we can, that Christ's law of righteousness may be established in this land, the righteousness that exalteth a nation; and that the sin which is a reproach to any people may be wiped out.

I.

MY DEAR SON:—Twenty-one years ago to-day you were born into this world. It was a day of great gladness to your mother and me. During all the long years that have elapsed, you have been the object of our fondest love, and most anxious care. Your shortcomings have caused us the most profound grief; your success and Christian character and conduct, the deepest gratitude and joy. To-day you cease to be a boy, and become a man. Not only really but legally. Deeply interested as I am in you, I felt that I could not let the day pass without marking it by some special communication. Had I money to give, gladly would I endow you with wealth. But "silver and gold have I none, yet such as I have" I freely give.

You are a professed Christian, and I hope a real one. It would hurt me more than I can tell, to think you were not. Now,

1. Keep close to Jesus; trust him; follow him; obey him; come what may, be loyal to him.

2. Never omit prayer, morning and evening, on any account. Be afraid of no one. You come of a

praying family, on both sides, for generations. Your heritage is many prayers. When you have a home, keep up the honored customs of family worship. Let no company or crowd of business prevent it. Remember the Sabbath day to keep it holy. Go to church regularly: wet or dry, cold or hot, be in your place. Make the very most of the services. At home, give the day to the Bible and religious reading, such as will make you better. Put out of the way everything secular.

3. Aim to be an active, useful Christian. Do your part in the prayer-meeting, Sabbath-school, and the business of the church. Never let it be said that —— is of no account. Be sure that you always count one.

4. Always, everywhere, at all times, be on the side of truth and righteousness. Never permit yourself to be in an equivocal position. Never permit yourself to be on the wrong side of any question.

5. Keep clear of all use of intoxicating drinks. Never taste them, not even wine or beer. Keep clear of all games of chance. Have nothing to do, that you can possibly help, with men that drink or gamble. All companionship with them will corrupt you and damage your reputation.

6. You have chosen your profession; stick to it, determined to fight it out on that line. Keep your

eye on the top; if you are a diligent student and improve your opportunities, you will in time plant your feet there. This is the way to win, but remember you must know before you can do; therefore, study, *study*, STUDY.

7. Manage your finances wisely. Keep out of · debt. Pay as you go. Let no man tempt you to run into debt, then year by year be hand-cuffed and shackled. But I cannot add more. I might write a volume, but why? We are well and happy. —— came last night with her boy. We have a merry time. Baby voices are heard constantly. The children are wonderfully pleased. Come when you can. You are always welcome to your father's house. The Lord bless thee and keep thee.

Your affectionate father,

DAVID A. WALLACE.

II.

MY DEAR SON.—Although I have not heard from you since I last wrote, I feel like writing to you again this morning. I am very busy; still I feel that I must take time to write to you. Your welfare is very dear to me. I exceedingly rejoice in it. Misfortune to you I feel as keenly as to myself. I want to say something to you about your religious interests to-day. You have made a profession of faith in Christ. I trust your profession was genuine, and that you are a child of God. Be faithful in reading the Bible, and in private prayer. Let your room be a Bethel. Wherever you are, select a church. Make it for the time your own. Attend its prayer-meetings. Help in its Sabbath-school. Go to all its public Sabbath services. A poor church and preacher is better than none. You will get good by going, and you will suffer loss by staying at home. I very much desire that you remain a member of the United Presbyterian Church. My first reason is, that I believe before God it to be more nearly right than any other; and it will be very gratifying to both mother and me. Fix a certain percentage of your income and pay it out for the Lord's cause. Be faithful to your convictions of truth and duty. Stand up for your principles. A reputation as a man of principle is of incalculable value in this world. Always keep a clear conscience. There is more happiness in that than you can tell. " Be faithful unto death, and I will give thee a crown of life." Yours affectionately,

DAVID A. WALLACE.

III.

MY DEAR SON.—You are now in a fair way to get along. I trust the Lord will bless you and prosper you. I do not want to annoy you by a lecture; but I will put down a few things which you will notice:

1. Never, at any time, do anything your conscience condemns. Keep a clear conscience. It will never pay to defile it.

2. Be faithful to your God and Saviour. Come what may, neglect no religious duty. Always be on the Lord's side.

3. Study economy, yet be generous in giving.

4. Be faithful to the interests of your employers. Never neglect or slight any work committed to you. When men trust you, be sure and prove worthy of the trust.

5. Learn all you can. Study to do your best to get on.

Now, my dear boy, think on these things. I will trouble you no more with admonitions. You have been told enough. Now, my heart's desire and prayer to God is, that you may develop into an intelligent, able, successful Christian. You cannot tell how near you are to our hearts. Any mishap befalling you would break them. Come and see us when you can, but business first.

Your father,

DAVID A. WALLACE.

My Dear Friend:—Understanding that you are about to leave home for college, I have decided to write you this letter, for the purpose of making a few suggestions which you may find valuable. The world which you are about to enter, is in many respects different from that in which you have moved. College will be to you a blessing or a curse. You may make it the one or the other. Earnestly desiring your welfare I drop you these lines.

The aim of the college is the physical, mental and moral improvement of the student. Its course of study, means and methods are all arranged with the view of securing these ends. Just in proportion as you become a healthier, stronger, more intelligent, sharper, wiser, better man will you attain the ends of the college. The course of study is arranged with the view of securing mental and moral culture. Pursue it carefully, make thorough work of it, master it. Do not make study secondary and something else primary. Do not study for a degree merely, nor for the reputation of scholarship, but for excellence. All the regulations of the college have been arranged with the view of securing its ends most effectually in the improvement of the

14 (209)

student. They have been adopted, only after the most careful consideration. They are commonly the result of a very large experience. Observe them carefully. Do not despise them. You cannot disregard them without hurt. Students suffer great loss when they trample college rules under foot. Remember also that physical excellence and moral excellence are ends as valuable to you as mental excellence. Be careful not to prosecute your studies so as to ruin your health; be careful not to neglect moral and spiritual culture. You will have made poor use of the opportunities of the college if you graduate with a body made worthless by disease or with a moral character wrecked by vice. Aim at all excellence, and work for it as wisely and earnestly as you can.

In your intercourse with the professors, treat them as gentlemen. Act yourself as a gentleman. There is nothing much more contemptible in a student than insolence to a professor or instructor. Submit implicitly to their authority. Never resist it. Never conspire with other students to overthrow it. It is wrong. In the end, whatever success may attend your plans for a time, you will be defeated, and suffer more than you at the time may think probable. When you cannot be an obedient, orderly student, leave. You are not under obligations to remain a day in the college; but you are under obligations to be studious, orderly, gentlemanly while you do remain. Treat the professors as your friends. If you need advice, go to one of them. If you are in trouble, select a professor, tell him all about it, and he will be able and willing to help you much.

Be courteous and gentlemanly in all your intercourse with your fellow students. Be more ready to give than ask a favor. Avoid tale-bearing. Never circulate an evil report. When asked to join in anything you believe to be wrong, refuse promptly and decidedly. Let no sophistry entice you to do wrong. Be swift to hear, but slow to speak. Be courageous in standing up for your own convictions. Beware of all entanglements of every kind that might interfere with your standing up for the truth and the right. Don't permit any son of mischief to wheedle you into saying or doing anything wrong or ridiculous. If you do permit yourself to be fooled, keep it to yourself. Beware of proclaiming your own stupidity to the public. Let conscience and good common sense be your guide, and you will not go far wrong.

Remember that your money is given you by your father to meet your necessary expenses. You have no right to waste it. Send him a complete and exact account of your expenses every month. It is his right. If you make a foolish expenditure, tell him all about it. He knows a boy's wants and dangers, and will be ready to overlook the blunder. Cover up nothing from him. No matter what happens, let him know everything. It will give him unspeakable pleasure to know that you trust him and tell him all. In general, remember that you will never have any better friends than your father and mother. Honor them, trust them, do all you can to make them happy; they will do more for you than any other friends you will ever find.

I need not tell you to attend your own church regularly. Be a consistent Christian, an earnest Christian, an active Christian. Take your place in the Sabbath-school at once. If you are not needed as a teacher, enter the Bible class, and make all you can out of it. You will find many earnest Christian men at college. Become intimate with them. You may get much good from them. In all respects, study to grow in grace, and in the knowledge of Christ.

But my sheet is full and I must close. May the Lord bless you and make you a blessing.

Yours affectionately, D. A. W.

TO A THEOLOGICAL STUDENT.

I.

DEAR FRIEND:—The time is drawing near when you will enter formally on the study of theology, as preparatory for the office and work of a minister of the gospel. This is a very important era in your life. It is hardly possible for you to pass through it without more than ordinary thoughtfulness. My object is to suggest to you a few things worthy of your attention just now:

Be sure you are a true believer in the Lord Jesus Christ. Without this assurance you will have but little enjoyment in your work either as a student or a minister. But fully persuaded that you have been born again; that you are in Christ; that you are a saint of the Most High; that you have been called and justified; that you are a child of God and an heir of heaven, you will find the work of preparation full of pleasure. And when you enter on the active duties of the ministry, it will be with unspeakable satisfaction. Settle this question once for all. Take your place as a son in the family of God, beside your elder brother, and then press forward towards the most complete preparation and the highest service.

In settling this question, you will find Erskine's sermons on "Faith and Assurance" and Bonar's "God's Way of Peace" very valuable.

Be sure that you have been called of God to serve him in the gospel of his Son. You know that it is the prerogative of the Lord Jesus to call into his service whom he will. You may be a Christian and yet never have been called to the ministry. Without evidence of such a call, you can never have any assurance of God's presence with you or blessing upon you. Assured that you have been separated unto the gospel of God, you can confidently claim the promises made to his servants. Resting on these you will go forward confident of his presence with you wherever he may send you, and confident too that his own word preached by you will not return unto him void. Settle this question also, so completely that it will need be raised no more. If you do not fully understand the subject talk it over with your pastor, and with your professor of theology after you reach the seminary. Make thorough work of it. Undecided as to your call to the ministry, you will have but little comfort in it.

The great work of the theological student is to make himself fully acquainted with the mind of God as expressed in the Holy Scriptures. To this end you must study the Bible with special care. Master the Greek and Hebrew originals. Whatever effort

it may cost you to read your Hebrew Bible and
Greek Testament with ease put it forth. Let this be
your chief work until completed. Aim by careful
and patient study fully to master the written word;
seek the presence and gracious influences of God's
spirit while you study. Drawing your theology di-
rectly from the Bible it will have a freshness, clearness, and fulness, otherwise unattainable. However
carefully you study systems and treatises, let the
word of God have your chief attention.

As yet you have done but little at investigation.
Your principles have been adopted for the most part
with but little study. Aiming to become a teacher
of others, to answer inquiries that may be put to you,
and solve difficulties that will be pressed on your
attention, you must now, while a student of theology,
subject your principles to the most rigid scrutiny.
Take up each subject separately, examine it carefully
and patiently. Consider the evidences on which each
principle rests, and the objections that may be made
to it; the evidence on which the opposite principle
rests and its difficulties. Examine the subject as a
whole, and in all its parts. Do not rest satisfied
until you have explored every inch of the ground. I
have found the following plan of study very satisfactory: Take a particular doctrine, " Justification "
for example. First collect and write down all the
Scriptures that bear upon it. Examine each text

and ascertain its exact meaning. Then draw out from all these a statement of the doctrine as you have found it, as logically as you can. Next examine the declarations of the Confession and Testimony on the subject and compare them with your own conclusions. Then select the best treatise you can find, defending each of the great positions taken on the subject. Read these works with the greatest care. After you have mastered them, then look up the history of the doctrine. At every step you will become more familiar with the subject, and finally you may expect to be fully persuaded as to the truth. Such an investigation will so root, ground, settle and establish you, that you will not be shaken and tossed by every wind of doctrine. It will give you confidence, decision, earnestness. I know of but few more pitiable sights than a professed minister of the gospel, who has never investigated the principles which he teaches, afraid to affirm anything, trembling when the gainsayer opens his lips. But, how grand the man who knows whereof he speaks; who, confident in the positions which he has taken, is prepared to defend them successfully, assail them who may. At every step in such investigations you will find your professors invaluable helps. They have gone over the ground before you and can give you the most valuable aid. Don't despise it. You will find this hard work indeed, but exceedingly profitable. I have no fears of this thorough research making you dissatisfied with the principles of our church; it will establish you rather. But your time must not all be spent in study. You must give special attention to the state of your own heart, and hence you must spend much time in reading, prayer and meditation, with special reference to your spiritual nourishment. You must remember, too, that you will learn best how to do the Lord's work by doing it. Hence in the Sabbath-school, the prayer-meeting, and in more public places, as opportunity offers, speak out for Christ, and do the best work in his service you can. Go among the sick and troubled, and learn the work of a son of consolation. Go among men and women, living in sin, and learn how to win such to Christ. Thus exercising your gifts you will fast become a workman that needeth not to be ashamed.

But I must stop. Think on the things I have written. Go to work determined to succeed. My heart's desire and prayer to God is that he may be with you and bless you, and that you may be made a blessing to the church and the world.

Your friend,   D. A. W.

II.

DEAR FRIEND:—Yours of the 24th ult., asking me to "tell what constitutes a call to the gospel ministry, or what are the evidences of it," has been received. I cheerfully comply with your request.

There is an external and an internal call to the ministry. The former is given by the church. It does not give fitness for the work. The church examines those who profess to have been called of God, and in ordination, orders and acknowledges them as duly authorized to do the work of the ministry. The external call proceeds upon and presupposes the internal, which is of God. To this I ask special attention:

I. The Lord calls into the ministry only the godly. He selects those whom he would have serve him in the gospel from among the converted, the believing loving and obedient. He does not send the unconverted, the unbelieving and the disobedient. Those whom he calls to his service have strong faith in the Lord Jesus Christ as a personal Saviour. The love of Christ constrains them to do what they can for the promotion of his cause; the love of souls impels them to do what they can to win sinners from sin and hell back to Christ, to holiness, to heaven. But all the godly are not called to the ministry, not even all in whom these graces of the Spirit may be in vigorous and lively exercise. There is a special call.

II. The elements of this call are, I think, as follows:

1. A desire to be engaged in the work of the ministry, a liking for it. Not a liking for public

speaking merely, nor a liking for the consideration that attaches to the ministerial office; nor for the positions and emoluments that may be won in its exercise, nor for any of its accessories merely, but for the work itself. This desire should be a constraining desire, such as will move one towards it; a considerate desire that remains after counting the cost fully; a disinterested desire for the service and not for the honors and rewards that attend it in this world; an earnest desire, and not a mere feeble, indefinite liking; an abiding desire, and not a desire that will pass away like the morning dew. Such a desire exists in no heart in which it has not been wrought by the Holy Spirit. It is not of man, but of God. When a young man finds such a desire rising in his heart, remaining and strengthening, he has, I think, evidence that God is calling him to this service.

2. But when the Lord calls he also qualifies, and hence I believe that fitness for the ministry is a second element in a call. Paul, in his first Epistle to Timothy. 3: 2-7, gives the necessary qualifications at length. Until a man finds himself to be in some good degree in possession of these attainments, his call is not complete. He is not yet authorized to apply for admission to the ministerial office. The church is not yet warranted in recognizing him as called of God, and in ordaining him by the laying on the hands of the presbytery.

The call is in progress, but not complete. And here I desire you to give special attention to " aptness to teach." This, I think, implies two things— (1.) Native talent, natural ability; such as with due culture will enable one to comprehend and expound gospel mysteries. (2.) Learning, acquaintance with these truths; so that he can explain them to those who desire to hear them. One who finds himself in possession of sufficient natural ability, in addition to the desire described above, is warranted in seeking that intellectual culture, that knowledge and understanding of things, secular and sacred, that will enable him to help men and women to a better understanding of the things concerning the kingdom of God. Before, however, anyone can decide the question of his " aptness to teach," he must have, by actual trial, determined whether or no he possesses this qualification. A man may be a genius of the highest order, be distinguished for the extent and accuracy of his theological scholarship, and still be far from " apt to teach." This I regard as a special attainment made by comparatively few. It should not, therefore, be taken for granted, but its existence should be demonstrated by careful experiment in teaching.

I have, you will perceive, given you but two elements of a call to the ministry, but my sheet is full. Next week I shall direct your attention to a third.

Yours affectionately.   D. A. W.

III.

DEAR FRIEND:—In my last I mentioned two elements of a call to the ministry—a desire for the work, and the necessary qualifications for it.

3. There is, however, a third which should not be overlooked. I mean opportunity. There may be this desire, there may also be native talent and no insuperable mental or moral disqualifications but opportunity may be lacking, and, as long as this is the case, a call cannot be regarded as complete.

The opportunity may be lacking to acquire the necessary culture. The money needful may not be attainable, or the inquirer may be under such obligations to others that he cannot give himself to the work of preparation. God does not require a man to enter the ministry until he first gives him opportunity to prepare for it. If a young man is conscious of the desire which constitutes the first element of a call, conscious of possessing native talent sufficient, conscious of no insuperable disqualification, and still lacks the opportunity referred to above, let him wait patiently. If God desires his service in the ministry, he will open up the way.

But the needed learning may have been acquired, and opportunity still be lacking to enter on the work of the ministry. Existing obligations may keep the inquirer in other work, or the door may be shut so that he cannot enter in. God does not call on men to break, disregard, or be unfaithful to existing obligations. When it is his pleasure that they should enter into a new branch of his service, he sets before them on open door, which no man can shut.

When these three things exist in the case of any man of God, I think he may regard his call as complete. If he desires to be engaged in the work, with a constraining, considerate, disinterested, earnest, abiding desire: if he possesses the qualifications described by the apostle; if full opportunity has been afforded him, then he may regard himself as not only really and truly, but fully and completely, called of God to the ministry of the word. He not only may go forward, but it is at his peril that he holds back. Let him submit the evidences of his call to the elders of the church; it then becomes their duty, being satisfied of its validity, to ordain him to the work of the ministry, and to certify him to the church and to the world as one called of God. He can go forth claiming the promises and rejoicing in his work. .

And here I ask your attention to the following earnest words from an "Address to Students of Divinity," by the famous John Brown, of Haddington. I find it prefixed to his "System of Theology," a work which ought to be in the library of every

minister and student of theology, but of which I
have never seen but a single copy. He says: "Take
heed that your call from Christ and his Spirit to
your ministerial work be not only real, but evident.
Without this you can neither be duly excited or
encouraged to your work; nor hope, nor pray for
divine success in it; nor bear up aright under the
difficulties you must encounter, if you attempt to be
faithful. If you run unsent by Jesus Christ and
his Spirit, in the whole of your ministrations you
must act the part of a thief and a robber, a
pretended and treacherous ambassador of Christ
and his Father, and a murderer of men's souls, not
profiting them at all. What direction, what support,
what assistance, what encouragement, what reward,
can you then expect? Ponder, therefore, before
God. Have you taken this honor to yourselves? or
were you called of God as was Aaron? Has Jesus
Christ sent you to preach the gospel, and laid upon
you a delightful and awful necessity to preach it?"
These are weighty words, and demand your serious
consideration. One thing more: Do not be in haste
to complete your theological studies. Take plenty
of time. Make thorough work. Be sure you are
familiar with your Hebrew Bible and Greek testament. Go to the bottom of the great questions
that will often rise and demand an answer. See
that you are well established in the faith, that you

fully understand it, and can make its principles plain. By work in the prayer meeting Sabbath-school and elsewhere acquire all possible "aptness to teach," so that when you enter on official duty you may be a workman that needeth not to be ashamed.

Praying that the richest blessings of a covenant-keeping God may descend and rest upon you, I remain, Yours affectionately,

D. A. W.

TO A YOUNG MINISTER.

I.

DEAR BROTHER:—I see in the papers that you have been ordained to the office of a minister of the gospel and installed as pastor of a congregation of Christian people. I have thought that I could give you some hints in respect to your work which would be valuable to you, and hence I write you at this time.

Your work as a preacher is to teach men the gospel of the grace of God. You may, on different occasions, give men instruction on other subjects, but this does not belong to your ministerial work. I have no hesitation in saying that you should confine yourself to this grand old subject. In illustrating and expounding the way of salvation through Jesus Christ you will find ample scope for all your powers, and enough to do to occupy all your time.

In respect to the gospel, I desire to impress upon your attention the importance of ascertaining precisely what it is, and of placing it before the people with the utmost fulness and clearness. One would think that the most careless reader of the Bible

15 (225)

could not fail to know the gospel exactly. Yet, if you will talk a little with Christian people of average intelligence, and note carefully statements which you will see in print and hear from the pulpit, you will find prevalent very indistinct and inadequate views of the subject. The preacher undertakes to prescribe for the spiritual diseases of his people, and he ought to make his prescription correct in every particular. Study the subject carefully. Go to your Bible. Examine every scripture that bears on the gospel, every illustration of it. every allusion to it. Be sure that you have the full Bible doctrine. Beware of taking a part for the whole; of confounding things that differ, and of making distinctions where there is no difference. Study carefully the expositions which the great lights of the Christian church have given of it. Rest content only when you are assured that you have found the truth, and the whole truth on the subject. Having found it, use all diligence to teach it clearly to your people. If you adopt the methods of statement and illustration employed by any one writer, your preaching will become tame and uninteresting from sameness. If, however, you vary your modes of presentation to set forth the gospel in all the forms, under all the aspects, and with all the variety of the Scriptures themselves, your preaching will constantly be new and interesting. The more closely you follow the Bible, the more varied will your preaching be.

There are certain questions connected with the gospel which trouble many serious people. Among them one of the most prominent is, assurance of salvation. We do not desire to live in doubt, we desire peace, confidence, hope. We all shrink from living a life of anxiety in respect to our interest in Christ. As soon as you gain the confidence of your people, and they begin to speak freely to you, you will find that this question gives many much trouble. In order to be prepared to help inquirers, you must master the subject thoroughly. You must not only learn the truth as it is presented in the word of God, but you must yourself live in the enjoyment of that peace that passeth all understanding. If you have not attained it, you will be but a poor guide to others. Being justified by faith, having peace with God, and rejoicing in the hope of glory of God, you will be able to lead others successfully into the same land of light and joy. Early in my ministry I was much troubled with this question. Through the instructions of the fathers of our church (some of whom have fallen asleep), and the writings of Erskine and Anderson, I was led to a full comprehension of the truth, and I feel sure that afterwards my preaching and intercourse with inquirers was much more effective for good. You may rest assured, my dear brother, that you will be far from doing the work which you may and ought to do, if you do not attain to clear and correct views of this subject, and to that habitual peace with God which ruled in the hearts and minds of primitive Christians. But I must close. Yours fraternally,

D. A. W.

II.

DEAR BROTHER:—A few things of great importance additional to what I wrote the other day have suggested themselves to me.

"The law is our school-master to bring us unto Christ, that we might be justified by faith." Men do not apply to a physician until they feel themselves to be sick. The more deeply they are impressed with the dangerous character of their disease, the more promptly and earnestly do they seek some one who can cure them. Men do not seek Christ, they do not feel any personal interest in the gospel until they feel that they need a Saviour. They do not feel that they need a Saviour until they feel themselves to be sinners, guilty, condemned, helpless; children of wrath and heirs of hell. They do not feel themselves to be sinners until they understand something of the high claims of the law under which they live, and God's infinite holiness and justice. In God's perfect law, in the light of that commandment which is exceeding broad, men may see themselves as God sees them—dead in trespasses and in sins. Hence, in bringing men to Christ we must preach the law. We must unfold it in all its grandeur, authority, purity and spirituality; we must exhibit God as holy and just; we must help men to see that sin is an abominable thing in God's sight: and that because of the sin that is in them the wrath of God abideth on them. We must, however, be careful not to preach the law as a way of life, or as a covenant of works. Men are prone to seek life by obedience to the law. One of the first movements of the convicted sinner is to reform his life, mend his ways, become a better man, and thus secure God's favor. We must, however, press on them the utter hopelessness of obtaining salvation in this way; they cannot come up to the requirements of his most holy law, and if they could, there is no satisfaction which they can possibly make for the sins of the past. We must so preach the law as to drive men from it as a way of salvation, and bring them to Christ, who is the end of the law for righteousness to every one that believeth. If we lead men to rest in the law, we deceive them; if they are not driven from it to Christ they perish.

The first and great work of the gospel minister is to bring souls to Christ. The inquiring sinner, crushed under a load of guilt, needs Christ at once. We should point him to the Lamb of God, and exhort him to flee to him without a moment's delay. We should put nothing between the inquirer and Christ. We should put every obstacle out of his way. We should by all means help him to the only Saviour. He may reform his life. he may make a personal profession of faith, he may take his place with the people of God in all worship and all service, and still, if he is not in Christ, he is a child of wrath still under the curse. Hence, in this way do all you can to bring sinners to the Saviour.

The believer is one with Christ, he is justified, a saint, a child of God, an heir of heaven, a king and a priest unto God, a temple of the Holy Ghost. Once in Christ he is with Christ in heavenly places. In preaching godly living to a Christian people, I think it is a matter of great importance to lead them to look upon themselves as justified, as children, saints, kings and priests. This done, with what tremendous power comes the apostolic exhortation to walk worthy of the vocation wherewith we are called. If we are saints, certainly it is fitting that we should live as becometh saints, and this certainly includes holiness in all manner of conversation. If he has done so much for us, redeemed us with his own blood, raised us up together with himself, and made us sit together with him in heavenly places, surely it is fitting that we trust him implicitly, love him supremely, and serve him devotedly, walking in all his commandments and ordinances blameless. In developing these grand themes intended for the perfecting of the saints, your preaching will be in no danger of becoming tame and uninteresting. There will be no sameness about it if only you exhibit the truth in all the varied forms and relations, and with all the varied illustrations which we find in the Bible.   Yours fraternally.

D. A. W.

III.

DEAR BROTHER:—In addition to your duties as pastor and teacher you also sustain the relations of an elder, and hence have work to do in the management of the affairs of the church.   As an elder you are on a footing of perfect equality with the other members of the session.   You are officially neither the inferior nor the superior of any one of them, except in this, that, according to the provisions of our Book of Discipline, you are the permanent moderator of your session, and hence enjoy the peculiar rights which belong to this office.   In the Presbytery, the Synod, and the Assembly, the ruling elder, as we call him, is your official equal.   His rights and privileges in all matters of government are identical with your own.   In the church courts you are an elder and nothing more.

This being the case, it is evident that you have no right to control your session, unless you can do it by virtue of superior wisdom and intelligence.

It is not for you any more than for another elder to force your views on the session, and crowd them through whatever the other members may think. You are quite a young man; you have had absolutely no experience in the performance of the duties of an elder; you have formed certain notions as to what ought to be and what ought not to be in a congregation. Some of these notions are doubtless very good, but some of them are likely to be very crude. In five years from now they will be very much modified, and you will be disposed to smile at many things which you may now think are very wise. Still more, plans and methods which worked admirably in another congregation, with different elders, and among a people in many respects very different from yours, might be very unsuitable in your church. Besides, your session contains some men of great piety, wisdom and intelligence, who have long and large experience as elders, and who understand the peculiarities of the people perfectly. It would, it seems to me, be but little short of impertinence in you to go before that session with new plans and methods, determined to force them through. You may succeed. Many of them will be loth to offend you or unwilling to oppose a measure on which you seem to be set, and acquiesce, yet their judgments not be convinced. You cannot expect such men to co-operate very heartily in carrying out measures of whose wisdom they are in doubt. Without their co-operation you will be in danger of failure. Failure would bring mortification to yourself and destroy your influence with your people; crimination and recrimination would inevitably follow, and when such a state of things exists the pastoral relation is not likely to be very permanent. I am fully persuaded that young ministers leave the congregations in which they first settle, at so early a day, chiefly for this reason.

It is your duty to study carefully the circumstances and wants of your people, and to devise ways and means for the promotion of their spiritual welfare. Whatever your plans may be, bring them before your elders as suggestions. If you bring them forward as measures in relation to which your own mind is fully settled, and take the place of an advocate, you forestall free discussion. Opposition to them will look like opposition to you. You will not be likely to learn all the facts bearing on the case. If, however, your views are submitted as queries or suggestions, the way is open for full and free discussion; if time is taken to deliberate, you will come to see that your views are not wise, or ill-timed, and the way will be open for you to drop the matter altogether, or postpone it to a more convenient time. Or, your elders will be fully persuaded of the soundness of your opinions, cordially adopt

them and do their utmost to carry them out. If
they succeed, your policy becomes permanent; if
they fail, the elders, all together, bear the responsibility. I have found, in many localities, men of
wonderful wisdom among the eldership. They are
commonly modest men, and yet men of unbounded
influence in the neighborhood. If you study carefully the character and standing of the members of
your session, you will likely find one or more from
whom you may learn much, and who, if cordially
sustaining you, will be to you a tower of strength;
if against you, you will remain where you are but a
short time. Look out such men. Become familiar
with them. Draw them out. Learn their views
and feelings. Talk over with them your plans and
schemes. Find out their opinions about them.
Be very sure you are right; be very sure of the support of the other elders and of the people; if you
decide to act contrary to the convictions of such
men, carefully reconsider the whole matter, and
take plenty of time for it before you come to such a
conclusion. Wishing you a successful pastorate, I
remain, Yours fraternally,
D. A. W.

IV.

DEAR BROTHER:—There is a prevailing feeling
that the whole work of the preacher must be performed in the pulpit. Hence, many, to a great

extent, excuse themselves from the more private preaching. This, however, is not according to apostolic practice. Paul in his address to the Ephesian elders speaks of having taught "publicly and from house to house," and of "warning every one, night and day, with tears. "Thus he labored in the gospel of God. The most successful ministers in all ages have followed his example in this thing. My own observation has satisfied me that no part of one's ministry is so effective as the personal dealing of man with man. He who neglects it, fails to use one of the most important elements of power. Let me, therefore, press on you the importance of doing your utmost to attain excellence in this department of your work. Study it. Pray for wisdom, strength and grace to help you in it. Talk with old ministers about it, and avail yourself of the lessons of their experience. At first you may fail; but do not be discouraged; try again and again, with the fixed determination not to fail, and at last success will crown your efforts. Guard against frivolity when among your people. Do not fall into the habit of making all your visits merely social. In this way we are in danger of wasting many hours and days of precious time. Aim to know the views and feelings of every one of your people. Be specially attentive to the young. You may set it down as a fact, that every young man and woman, yes, every boy and

girl old enough to think in your charge, who has
not been brought to Christ, is interested in spiritual
things. Young people are commonly timid. They
shrink from speaking of these things and yet long,
many times with an unutterable longing, to unbosom
themselves to some one in whom they can trust and
who can help them. Cultivate their confidence.
Talk kindly to them. Beware of repelling them
with coldness or severity. It is your business to
take them by the hand and lead them to Jesus. Do
not neglect the sick; study how to cheer, comfort
and encourage them. Aim so to conduct your visits
that your words may do them good. To talk and
pray with the sick profitably is a very high attainment. Do not rest content until you have made it.
If you fail in this part of your work, you can hardly
be a success as a pastor, and you will have no very
strong hold on the affections of your people.

Be careful, however, that you do not fall into the
opposite and equally dangerous extreme of under-
valuing your pulpit work, and of giving almost exclusive attention to pastoral duties. It has been
said that feebleness in the pulpit is, in the estimation of his people, the unpardonable sin in a
preacher. However this may be, it exerts a tremendous influence in injuring his reputation and influence. On the contrary, a man who habitually
preaches ably, is all the more welcome in the homes

of his people, and at the bedside of the sick, and his words have all the greater weight when he talks in private to one whom he wishes to impress with the truth. Not unfrequently the remark may be heard, "Our minister is a good man, but——." His people love him and—pity him, not love him and honor him. Such a man's influence will not be very extensive. Be sure, therefore, that you take all necessary time to prepare for the pulpit. Keep up your habits of study. Give your forenoons to this work, unless unavoidably hindered. Let your people know that you desire the first half of every day to be uninterrupted, and they will respect your wishes. The afternoons will ordinarily be sufficient for pastoral work. Your congregation must be widely scattered indeed, if it is often necessary for you to leave home in the forenoon. Do not confine your reading to the subjects on which you are preparing a sermon. Your reading should take a much wider range and be much in advance of the subject to be discussed the next Sabbath. Never preach on a subject you do not fully understand. Never commence to write a sermon on a subject until you have carefully studied it and mastered it. I have found it work well to select my subjects weeks in advance, and to keep working them up ahead, so that when I come to prepare a sermon for the next Sabbath the work of investigation and arrangement has already been completed, and nothing remains but to write out or make an extended brief of matter already collected and arranged. But I must stop. Hoping that these hints may be profitable to you, I remain,

Yours fraternally,

D. A. W.

www.ingramcontent.com/pod-product-compliance
Lightning Source LLC
Chambersburg PA
CBHW020059030726
47498CB00006B/1868